Ophidian

A Willow and Birch novel

Jon Latham

Jon Latham Books

Ophidian

All Rights Reserved

Edited by: Ella Medler Editing

Cover design by: Elizabeth Mackey

Acknowledgements

A huge thank you to Ella Medler for having the talent to notice things I looked at twenty to thirty times and still missed. For her insight, criticisms and positive feedback that makes me want to be a better author.

Thank you to Elizabeth Mackey ---Elizabeth Mackey Graphic Design--- for finding the ideal cover for this novel.

Nope! I didn't forget you, the reader. You will never know how much an author appreciates your taking time out of your busy day to just read.

Are you ready?

Here's the story.

3

2

1

GO!

Blankenship

Gracie smacked her snooze button and kicked her feet out of the covers. She sat up on the side of the bed and shook her hands through her hair, yawning loudly, wiggled her feet into her bunny slippers, made her way to the kitchen and punched the on button for her brand-new Keurig. Then she began her preparations for her favorite part of waking up. The shower.

Just another day in the life, she thought. Another boring day in her boring life. She constantly believed there had to be something better than this. She gets up, goes to work, comes home, plays with her dog, Willie, texts a friend or two, goes to bed, and so on. Boring!

Showered, dressed and coffee in hand, she climbed into her Camry and headed off to the store. She knew Arnold would be there. Arnold was always there. He came in early every morning, put together the bank deposit from the previous day, ran it to the bank, and was almost always back before she opened for business.

Gracie was the only cashier. Oops. That is to say, she was the only customer-service representative during the day shift, but she was also responsible for restocking, cleaning and signing. She was also trained in doing the books, prepping the sales and merchandising the shelves. She was a Gracie of all trades, totally capable of running the store by herself, and usually did. Arnold would help when it got busy, but mostly he sat on his ass, reading up on the stock market.

Arnold was the owner and manager. The owner part, she could understand. The man did have money, but manager? He managed to drink coffee. He managed to read the paper. He managed to get a little handy once in a while, but managing the store? Gracie laughed. She looked at the car beside her and saw the man had seen her laugh and had a querulous look. She pried her mouth wide and crossed her eyes. He should be watching the stoplight, not her.

Gracie criticized herself for thinking Arnold to be 'handy'. His touches weren't inappropriate. They were, however, touches. Gracie didn't like being touched. Arnold would put his hand on her shoulder when he was talking to her, sometimes, but he did that with the guys, too. That was just the way Arnold was.

She didn't think she was OCD. She played with Willie all the time and didn't find a need to sanitize herself after. Unless she was about to eat. Then she would naturally wash up first. She liked things clean, but she was not obsessive about it. No, she wasn't OCD. Arnold was good to her. He was a good man and she shouldn't have thought that.

Gracie pulled into the parking lot in the back of the store and stopped next to Arnold's car, grabbed her lunch bag and coffee, locked up the car and proceeded to the back door. She inserted her key, and unlocked the door.

Walking in, she sat her lunch bag down in the office, along with her coffee, and went to the day's folder to check what Arnold was putting on sale today. She grabbed the file, her opening drawer, and walked through the backroom door, heading to the cash register. As soon as she passed through, she couldn't help but let out a laugh. Arnold had fallen asleep at the table.

Gracie activated the register, slid in her drawer and closed it loudly. Nothing. Didn't even cause him to stir. "Arnold, wake up. You have to get to the bank." Still nothing. She walked from behind the counter. Would she have to shake him after thinking she didn't like being touched herself?

"Arnold," she yelled. She passed between two shelving units and had a clear view of the table area. There was no money on the table. Had he already gone to the bank? She passed a promotional rack and froze.

"Oh, my God! Shit! Oh, my God!" Gracie ran back to the counter, picked up the phone and dialed 9-1-1.

"9-1-1, what's your emergency?"

"Help me," Gracie cried. "I think my boss is dead. There's blood everywhere."

Birch

Kris was already off to work, so with the kids having finished breakfast, Travis got them all set for school and loaded them in his beater. He remembered a time when this actually seemed like a chore. Something he could do without. After having been without the kids for too long a period, he now wasn't sure how he ever could have considered it a chore.

Travis had Kris and the kids back, and he had no intention of ever letting them slip away again. Last week had been his three-month anniversary. He'd received his emerald chip and he placed it with the others in the holder that his supportive wife had spent a good deal of painstaking time hand-crafting for him.

Crafting was his wife's passion, but it didn't take away from how proud he was to display it on top of the dresser he faced every morning. It became part of his morning routine now to rub each chip before he left the house.

He pulled up in front of the school and watched as each of his children unbuckled themselves and bolted from the car in an attempt to catch their friends up. Much to his delight, there were always two 'I love you, daddy's', before the bolt. He watched and smiled as they ran up the steps to meet with their respective besties.

Travis pulled away from the curb and was nearly side-swiped by another parent who was obviously in a hurry to be in a hurry. *Take it easy, lady. You're talking seconds here.* He drove the four blocks back home and realized he wasn't nearly as animated a driver as he once was. He could only guess that to be an additional benefit of sobriety. The headaches were gone, too.

It was still well over an hour before he had to be at work, so on arriving home, he poured himself a cup of coffee and opened the cupboard to make himself a bowl of cereal. There was cereal in the cupboard, now. Not too long ago there wouldn't have been room for any cereal boxes. It would have been loaded with scotch, gin and vodka.

He sat down at the table and, while he was eating and enjoying his coffee, searched the already torn apart newspaper for the sports section. Baseball season was over and the Giants were in need of outfielders. Hopefully, they were busy trying to obtain a free agent or two. Before he could even find it, his phone dinged. It was a text from the captain.

[Murder/robbery. Arnold's discount. Get there.]

He responded and at the same time wondered where Willow had spent the night. It sure would be nice not to have to drive to work and try to find a parking spot. Her car was in the shop, so she had taken the cruiser home. If she was at home. It wasn't all that out of her way, coming from home, but if she had stayed at Mark's, it would be. He decided to ask.

[Hey, Shiner. Where'd you sleep last night?]

[Kinda nosy, aren't you, Paunch?]

[Yup. Relentless, too. Where?]

[We can do this all day, if ya want. I was at the Gaudiers'. No, wait, Marci's. No, wait. . .]

[Geez, why ya gotta be like that? Can you save me a drive or not?]

[I'll be there in about 15. I was going straight to Arnold's, tho.]

[That's fine. See ya in 15.]

Travis opened the sports section and skimmed all the headlines but found nothing on the Giants. *Idiots. Hope they lose a hundred games.* He put the paper back together and set it on the coffee table. He sent a text to Kris, so she wouldn't freak out when she saw his car in the garage. He told her a beautiful blonde was picking him up and they were going to hang out. She sent a text back, saying Willow had better taste than that.

Properly insulted, he did a cursory walk through the house, picked up the kids' rooms and poured out his coffee, placing the cup and his cereal bowl in the dishwasher. He grabbed his badge, ID, Nine and Taser, and walked out the front door to wait for Willow. It wasn't much of a wait. She drove up before he even got to sit down.

"Hey, Will," he greeted as he entered the cruiser. "Thanks for this. Now I don't have to spend ten minutes finding a parking spot."

"No problem. This actually works out well. My car will be ready this afternoon and you can drop me off." "Well, good. You're still on for tonight, right?"

"I am. Are you bringing them over to my place, or do you want me to come to yours?"

"Doesn't matter. Your call."

"Okay. Their toys are all at your place, so I'll come to you. Where are you taking her?"

Travis looked at his partner. The temptation was just too great for him to pass up. "The Gaudiers'. No, wait. Kramer's. No, wait. . ."

Willow burst out in a great laugh. "Touché. I'll just ask Kris. She'll tell me."

"You do that. Have you been questioned by the FBI yet?"

"Not yet, but I can smell it. It smells just like that diamond engagement ring he hid behind the spices."

"You were snooping in his house?"

"Not snooping, really. I was looking for cinnamon one morning when it was my turn to fix breakfast, and bam!
There it was."

"Have you decided yet?"

"Oh, I'll say yes. I love the man."

"Hopefully, he loves you, too. I'd hate to have to get rough with him."

"If you'd have seen the ring, you wouldn't be saying that. I guarantee. It wasn't cheap."

When Willow turned the corner leading to Historical, she pulled over to the side and the two of them did a quick scan of the street scene to see if anyone was showing more interest than they should have of the police activity. Nothing was obvious. Words weren't necessary, so Travis exited the cruiser and watched as Willow drove off, past the scene to the next corner, where she parked the cruiser.

Travis crossed the street and watched Willow do the same at the other end. The two began closing in on each other, looking in windows to see if anyone was watching Arnold's. Both of the detectives knew the killer might be watching the investigation of his handiwork unfold.

Travis met Willow in the middle of the block and they both crossed the street and entered Arnold's. The glass pane nearest the door handle had been broken and CSU had already dusted for prints but weren't yet scooping broken glass from the floor inside.

Fenowicz and Jack were lifting the victim from a table and laying him on the gurney, with the black bag over

Jack's shoulder. Besides the three different CSU officers, there were also two first responders in the store. One of which was talking to a twenty-something woman. The two detectives headed that direction.

"My lead," Travis said. "You technically had the Manning case, so my turn. You handle the woman and the first responders. I'm going to look at the back door."

Sturgeon

"Don't go anywhere," Willow said to the officer. "I have a couple of questions." The officer nodded and moved off and joined his fellow officers, leaving the crying woman to Willow. She was sitting, so Willow went down on her haunches and began the interview.

"I'm sorry you walked in on such a scene, but if you feel up to it, I have a few questions. May I have your name?"

"Grace. . . Grace Blankenship. Everyone calls me Gracie."

"Okay. For the sake of being different, I'm going to call you Grace. Can you tell me exactly what you did when you got here?"

"I drove up and parked next to Arnold. There's not a lot of parking spots available, so we all park close together. I grabbed my lunch bag and coffee and unlocked the door and walked in."

"The door was locked then? You heard the tumblers?"

"Yes. I felt it more than heard it. The lock is old and a little stiff. I sat my bag and coffee down, grabbed the sale folder and my drawer and came out here and saw Arnold. I thought he had fallen asleep."

Grace began to struggle, so Willow waited a moment for her next question. "When did you notice he wasn't sleeping?"

"When I saw the blood. I had made a lot of noise and called his name, first, but he didn't respond, so I walked out to shake him awake and saw the blood. The money was gone, too."

"Did Arnold always count money at the table?"

"Every day. It's away from the door, so no one can see him counting. How did they know he was even there? You can't see that table from outside."

"We're going to work on that, Grace. You saw the blood. Is that when you called the police?"

"Yes. Right away. Not even a minute passed."

"So, how long would you say you were here before you saw the blood?"

"Five minutes. Tops."

"After you called the police, did you do anything else? Move anything? Touch Arnold?"

Grace reached down beside the chair and pulled up a Louisville Slugger. "I backed up against this wall and waited. They were here quick. Not more than two or three minutes. One of the officers took Matilda away from me," she said, shaking the bat. "And then the other one went in search of the guy, but he was gone."

"You didn't see anyone, did you, Grace? Why do you say 'he' was gone?"

"No. I just assumed, and probably shouldn't have. It could have been a woman."

"How many people work here, Grace?"

"There's six of us. Max and I are the only full-timers, though."

"Do you all have your own key?"

"Yes. We pretty much have to or Arnold would never go home. Would never have, I guess."

"Grace. I'm going to need a little more information from you. Are you okay waiting for a bit while I talk to my partner?"

"I guess if I'm not safe with all you here, I never will be. Can I put the closed sign up?"

"Not yet, Grace. If you can restrict yourself to this chair while we search, I'd appreciate it."

Grace nodded and Willow moved off to talk to the returned Travis. "Anything?"

Travis shook his head. "Nothing substantial. CSU is scraping up cigarette butts and some assorted wrappers.

No sign of forced entry at the back door. How about the girl?
Anything there?"

"I don't think so. Her grief seems pretty sincere. She thinks the killer came in through the front door. I didn't correct her. Your case. I'm afraid all the employees have a key, and there are six of them."

"We have suspects, though. It wasn't a random robbery. That's the good news. You ready for the bad?"

"You're going to tell me there's no surveillance video?"

"Nada. Not even an old-style VHS. I hate these historical sites." Travis walked toward the front door and Willow followed. He opened the door to the point where the glass met the door. Not wide enough for a person to pass through, but wide enough to swing something and break the glass. He stood there and looked at everything around the door, and focused his stare on a display of souvenir-type novelties.

"Did you guys dust these?" he asked the nearest CSU officer.

"I doubt it," the officer responded. "We can, if you want."

"Please," Travis said. "One of these was used to break the glass."

The CSU officer looked at Travis as if he was the brunt of a joke, so Willow spoke up, before Travis felt the need.

"Whoever killed the victim either had a key, or was already in the store, waiting. The glass doesn't cover enough area to have been broken from outside, and the victim was shot in the back from close range. The broken glass would have startled him and he would have turned, and there was a powder-like substance on his shirt."

"If the killer was here all night," Travis interjected, "he would have eaten something or drank something. We need a complete canvas on this one."

The officer moved off to get his equipment and Travis turned to Willow. "See if she has access to the employee files or knowledge of the victim's routine. There's a coffee shop across the street. Maybe he goes over there and shoots the bull with someone. See if she knows anything about his personal life, or former employees that might have held a grudge."

Willow headed back to the interview, leaving the visual to Travis.

Birch

Travis stepped outside the door and closed it. He put his head as close to the glass panes as he could, in an attempt to see the table. It wasn't visible. He walked to the edge of the store and found no gap between businesses, and repeated the process on the other end. He had already checked in the back.

He walked back in, interrupting Willow and her witness. "Do you have a ladder, Miss Blankenship?"

The woman handed him the key for the tool closet. He proceeded to the door and found two ladders, one extension and one step. He took the extension ladder out the back door and placed it securely, climbing to the roof. He walked the entire roof and found no access to the store.

He replaced the extension and pulled out the step ladder, walking it to the center of the store and climbed up, carefully lifting the ceiling tile. Using his flashlight, he scanned the entire rafter area and, once again, found no indication anyone had traversed the beams. He replaced the ladder, locked the door and returned the key.

He walked over to the food area and first checked the three coolers. They appeared to have been recently stocked, probably as part of the closing procedures last night. He walked the two snack aisles and found nothing that looked like it had been disturbed.

Next, he moved to the center of the store and turned all directions, looking for where he would hide himself, if he were the killer. He ruled out the backroom area, as that would have been the first place Arnold would have gone to retrieve the money from the safe. The only place that looked promising was a corner behind the coolers. He walked that direction. He found nothing visible to the naked eye, so he asked CSU to dust the side of the cooler and the wall. Being here all night was looking less likely.

He went again out the back door, nearly knocking over one of the still-scraping and sifting CSU officers. He found the dumpster enclosure and opened it, revealing two standard-sized dumpsters. He pulled both out of the enclosure and scanned the ground inside.

He opened the first dumpster. Surprisingly, it didn't reek. The majority of the trash was in plastic bags. He climbed up and in, lowering himself carefully. He began, one by one, picking up the bags and checking for holes. When he found none, he lowered the bag to the ground outside the dumpster. With only three bags left, he found what he was looking for. He switched gloves and picked up the small auto by the barrel. Garcia 380. No clip. He checked the chamber carefully. No round.

The serial number had been filed off. He pulled out his trusty Swiss army and began unscrewing the grips. He found the serial number and pulled out his phone.

"Research. This is Mary."

"Mary. Detective Birch. I have a Garcia 380 auto I need a run for. Are you ready?"

"Go ahead."

Travis read off the serial number and then hung up with research. He texted the info to Willow, in the event she hadn't already gotten to the 'Do you own a gun' question. He called over CSU to get an evidence bag and turned the gun over to them, going back to his search, now looking for an expended casing, a single round and a clip.

He found nothing more in the dumpster and no holes in any of the bags, so he jumped out, threw the bags back in and rolled the dumpster back into the enclosure. He opened the second dumpster and climbed in with the same careful nature. One of the bags had a hole punched through it, and he found the clip at the bottom of the dumpster.

He climbed back out, set the clip on the ground and opened the bag with the hole. One at a time he pulled every item from the bag, and he was rewarded for his efforts. One expended casing. Then, after removing a few more items, the round from the chamber. He called CSU back over and had them remove the two items from the bag. When they had everything tagged, he began tossing bags back into the dumpster and rolled it back into the enclosure.

Once again, he began thinking with the mind of a killer. He scanned the back lot, the alley, the lots adjacent, and thought he found where the killer would have hidden, awaiting Arnold. He walked to the area thick with foliage and began looking for signs of hiding. He found two heavy boot prints in a cluster of bushes. Heavy enough that whoever wore them would have been there for a while.

He had no flags with him, so he tied one of his gloves around a branch of the nearest bush. He looked at the pavement area around the bush but saw no signs of which way the boots had left the dirt. He looked, one at a time, at every residence, business and sidewalk, trying to decide where to begin canvassing. A 380 wasn't very loud, but it still should have been heard.

Travis called the captain, asking for community service officers, as many as possible, to meet him at the store. He got a positive response, so he made his way back to the store. He stopped with the two CSU officers and pointed out the gloved branch, explaining what he found there. Then he reentered the store.

He saw Willow still interviewing Blankenship and digging through files, so he went into the employee bathroom and looked up, down and around but found nothing useful. There wasn't much else he could check here, until Willow finished. She would have the info on Arnold being married, the employees, and everything else he needed to continue.

The first responders had left, the coroner had left. There was no one here now except Blankenship, Willow, CSU and himself. The first order of business was going to be notifying the family. The worst part of the job would be the first step. Then the digging would get intense.

While he was waiting for Willow to finish, he began briefing the community service officers. The captain had found three. He explained the questions he wanted asked. He told them what to look for when they received the answers, and then sent them on their way through the neighborhood.

Willow came out of the backroom lugging a large stack of files. Travis told Blankenship that as soon as CSU had her printed, she could call and have the door boarded, but no one else was to be in the building until he called her. When CSU left, she could lock up and go home.

Travis took the files from Willow and the two left the store and walked to the cruiser. He loaded the files in the trunk and himself in the passenger seat.

"Have your feelings changed about her?" he asked.

"I don't think she did it, Travis. If she did, she's the best actress in history."

"Well, let's get this over with and then head in. God, I hate this part of the job."

"I'll take the lead. I don't like it, either, but it will go better if she hears it from a woman, I think." Willow started the car and began the drive to give the news to the wife of Arnold Bayer.

Sturgeon

Willow tried to formulate the words in her mind that she would say to Mrs. Bayer. It was bad enough that she had to tell the woman of her husband's death, but there was also the reality of the situation that they had no firm person of interest. She and Travis had shared their respective interview and physical, and they both agreed that the killer must have had a key. He hadn't waited overnight in the store. They agreed on the conclusion for many reasons, including Travis having found the footprints out back.

This would be the first time Willow had to do this, but better her than Travis. Travis was just too hard-nosed. The man had practically no compassion in his voice, because he was always thinking that everyone he talked to was a suspect.

Travis may have found the murder weapon. In all likelihood it was the murder weapon, but one thing he had drilled into her during their talks was to never assume. The round that the doc would pull out of Arnold would match, though. The alternative was that someone threw away a gun for no reason.

She made the final turn onto the street of the Bayer address and she was amazed at how her heart was pumping. This sucked. There was no other way to think about it. What a horrible thing to have to hear. Especially from the police. It was bad enough from the doctor. At least with him, your loved one was already in the hospital. It still would be unexpected.

"You're sure you want to be the one to do this?" Travis asked as she pulled the cruiser to the curb in front of the house.

"No. I'm not. It is something I have to get used to, though, since I'm a homicide detective."

The two exited the cruiser and Travis waited for her on the curb. She led the way to the front door and rang the doorbell. She wanted to take a deep breath first, but why delay the inevitable? It's not going to go away if you ignore it. The door opened way too fast for Willow.

"Yes?" the middle-aged woman in jeans and sweatshirt said.

"Are you Mrs. Bayer?" Willow asked. "Mrs. Arnold Bayer?"

"Yes. What's this about?"

"Mrs. Bayer. I'm Detective Sturgeon and this is Detective Birch. Would it be all right if we came inside?"

The woman looked back and forth between the two detectives, opened the door and stood aside so they could pass over the threshold.

"Have I done something wrong?" she asked.

"No, ma'am," Willow answered quickly, "but if you could sit with us a couple of minutes, that we might speak with you?"

Mrs. Bayer directed them to the dining room table and asked if they would like water or coffee. When the detectives graciously declined, the woman took a chair on the opposite side of the table and continued to look back and forth between the two.

"Mrs. Bayer, there is no easy way to say this. I'm afraid I have some horrible news. We were called to Arnold's Discount this morning. . . Mrs. Bayer, I'm afraid your husband was shot this morning during a robbery."

Mrs. Bayer's eyes bulged and a look of shock covered her features. Willow's heart sank as she watched the reaction, but she steadied herself and delivered the cruncher. "I'm afraid he was deceased on our arrival."

"Ohhh." The woman's head lowered to the table and her arms covered her from view.

"I'm so sorry, Mrs. Bayer. Is there someone we can call for you?" Willow asked.

The woman was bawling hysterically, but Willow thought she heard the word sister, so she asked where she could find the number. No answer came, and Willow watched Travis dart around the house looking for tissues. He finally came back from the hallway carrying a box and sat it on the table in front of Mrs. Bayer. Willow asked again where to find the number.

Mrs. Bayer lifted her head. Her eyes were red and wet and her mascara was beginning to run. She took a tissue and reached in her pocket for her cell phone. She paged through her address book between sobs, found the number and hit send, putting the phone to her ear. She began rambling immediately, but there was no way anyone on the other end would be able to understand her sobbing words, so Willow stuck her hand out and Mrs. Bayer handed the phone over.

"Who am I speaking to, please?" Willow asked.

"Charlotte. Who are you and what's wrong with Barb?"

"Charlotte, I'm Detective Sturgeon. Carpel P.D. Would it be possible for you to come and stay with your sister for a bit? I'm afraid we've had to deliver some traumatic news."

"Jesus! What happened? Never mind. I'm on my way." The woman disconnected before Willow could even thank her. Willow sat the phone down, after switching it to recent calls, and turned it to face Travis. She walked around the table and put her arm around a still-sobbing Barb Bayer.

"Mrs. Bayer," Willow began, "no one at the store seems to know what time Arnold gets there. Do you know what time he left this morning?"

"I get up at five. He's always gone by then," she sobbed out.

"Has he said anything to you about stops he makes on the way?"

"No. Hardly anything's opened by then. Who would do such a thing?"

"We're going to do everything we can to find that out, Mrs. Bayer. Did he say anything to you lately about problems he was having? People he was having trouble with?"

"No. As far as I know, everyone liked him. Even his employees. Why are you asking these questions? I thought you said it was a robbery."

"It may have been. In all probability, it was. We are going to be thorough, though. We want to find the person who did this. We'll investigate all possibilities. Dig for every lead we can."

Tires screeched outside. Travis went to the door. A woman was running toward the house. He let her in but stopped her charge to explain what happened. Charlotte's hands covered her mouth and she charged on, placing her sister in a crunching hug.

Willow got as much information out of Charlotte as she could, but she had begun mimicking her sister's sobs.

"We'll keep you as informed as possible, Mrs. Bayer. We'll be in touch. Once again, we're so sorry for your loss." Willow gathered Travis and the two left the sisters to their grief and headed back to the cruiser.

"You did well, Willow," Travis said when they were seated in the cruiser. "How are you, though?"

"Damn, that is miserable. How long do you normally allow before you start to interview the spouse?"

"Usually, I leave it for last, and then only if I haven't already got the answers I was looking for."

"Then I hope we have it solved by then. What a horrible thing to be told." She started the engine and pulled away from the curb, heading for the station. "Was there anything that looked promising on the phone?"

"There was one number. I wrote it down and will call it later. It was an area code on the coast. What time is your car going to be ready?" Travis asked, changing the subject to get her mind off what she'd just gone through.

"After four," she answered absently.

Birch

Travis hopped from the car when they got back, made his way in and turned immediately to the right and down the stairs to the coroner. Willow was on his heels. He knocked and was let in by Jack. Travis punched Jack's arm lightly, and then moved on to Doc.

"Hey, Doc," Travis greeted. "Get the bullet out yet?"

"You really annoy me, Birch. You know that? Yes, I did. It's at the lab. The cause of death is the gunshot. It glanced off the spine and went through the center of the heart. He was dead instantly. Now get the hell out of here. I have work to do."

"Geez, crabby," Travis responded. "Fine. I'll go to breakfast and let you solve the crime."

"Good. How long does it take you to eat, so I know when to expect you back?"

Travis rolled his eyes, shook his head at Willow, punched Jack's arm again and went out the door with Willow following. He walked across the hall and entered the evidence lab. He stopped and scanned the entire staff of ten friggin' people working in this one department, trying to find one he recognized from the scene. He saw him and walked that way.

"Hey, who's handling the round and weapon?"

"Tara," the man said without lifting his head. Travis stared at him, putting his hands in his pockets.

"Not Abby, huh?" Travis asked, which caused the man to look up.

"We don't have an Abby," he said, and then with a look of understanding, "Yeah, that's very funny." The man just shook his head and went back to his microscope. Travis stood over him for a few seconds and then tapped him on the head.

"What's your problem?" the man asked angrily.

"My problem is, I don't know who Tara is, dumbass. In case you haven't noticed, you have ten people working here. That's more people than the entire detective bureau. Do you guys take a four-hour lunch, or what?"

"She's the one in the corner with the computer, and in case you haven't noticed, every one of these techs is busy. You only deal with one crime. One. We deal with them all. Is there anything else I can do for you, Mr. Personality?"

"You could get me a cup of coffee and a bagel. And that's Detective Personality," Travis said as he went to Tara's station.

The woman had a screen up for rounds and was measuring and making notes on a tablet.

"Are you Tara?" Travis asked. The woman sat her tablet down, stood, turned to Travis and stuck her hand out with a smile.

"Yes. What can I help you with?"

"I'm Detective Birch and this is Detective Sturgeon," Travis said, accepting the hand. "I know we mainly communicate via email, but I was just across the hall, so I thought I'd stop in. Do you by any chance have anything yet on the weapon or round?"

"The round pulled from the body is a 380. I haven't matched it up yet with the weapon, but I think that's probably going to be a given."

"Thank you very much, Tara. I'll wait for the rest. Any prints, by chance?"

"No. I'm sorry. It looks like he wore gloves."

Travis thanked the woman, got another smile, and he and Willow left the lab and proceeded to the V. They arrived at the bureau but were waved into the captain's office before they got to their desks.

"What are we looking at?" the captain asked.

"Looks like a robbery," Travis answered. "Smells like a robbery, feels like a robbery, but I don't think robbery was the motive."

"Of course, you don't," the captain said, shaking his head. "I know I'm going to regret this, but why?"

"He wasn't given a chance to hand the money over, which he probably would have done. He was shot in the back and then the money was taken, as if it was an afterthought."

"It was made to look like a robbery, Cap," Willow added. "The front window pane was knocked out but it was pretty obvious to us that it was done after the killing."

"An employee, then?" the captain asked.

"Looks like it," Travis answered. "We'll be talking to all of them. Hopefully, only one had a grievance." He turned to Willow. "Did the girl give any indication of an unhappy employee?"

"Quite the contrary," Willow answered. "According to her, Bayer was pretty well-respected."

"Well, someone wanted the man dead," the captain said. "Find out who. Be quick about it. I'm flying to Baltimore in two weeks, and you're going to be running the show until I get back."

"Are you going to see Missy?" Willow asked. "You can save me some postage."

"I'm sure I'll see her a time or two, but I'm not your mailman. Buy a stamp."

"Wow," Willow laughed. "Wife's got you in the doghouse, huh?"

"Get the hell out of my office. Both of you."

Travis and Willow left and went to the V, after sharing looks and smiles. Travis sat at his desk, opened a file for Bayer, opened an investigation report, skipped over a few lines to possibilities, and entered Mrs. Bayer's name, Blankenship's name, and then the rest of the employees' names from Willow's note pad.

Willow was going through the employee files, so he began filling in the victim's name, address, and the rest, leaving the motive line blank. He filled in every line he could and then emailed it to Willow. She would enter DOBs and socials from the employee files and then email it to research for background checks.

This should be a slam-dunk. There weren't that many possibilities. Thorough interviews, followed by an interrogation, should provide them with enough details to get the evidence necessary for a conviction.

Life was different for homicide detectives than it was for ADAs. For an ADA, everyone was innocent until proven guilty. For homicide, everyone was guilty until they provided an alibi of their innocence. Travis wasn't an ADA. It took a lot to convince him you were innocent, and even then, he still had his doubts.

His phone dinged. He checked it and saw it was a text from research on the serial number of the Garcia. It was registered. Email forthcoming.

"As soon as you get that email off to research, we have to go. I'll be getting an email in a minute or two with the info on the owner of the 380. Bring the files, so we can check if the owner is a next of kin to one of the employees."

"Nearly done. I'm on the last employee."

"Red Lobster," Travis blurted. Willow pulled out her phone, paged through and showed Travis a text. It was from Kris.

[He thinks he's taking me to Red Lobster, but he'll find out when he gets home that we're going to McCallister's]

"Shit! Pricey!" Travis said.

"You could always say no," Willow said with a smile. Travis just looked at her with raised eyebrows, causing her to laugh.

"I think we'll probably leave around six or six-thirty. Will that give you enough time to get your exercise in for the day?"

"Oh, yeah. Plenty. Shower, too. Am I feeding the troops?"

"Good on the shower part," Travis said, receiving a smile and nod. "We'll have dinner started for you and the kids before you get there. I can't guarantee it will be ready, though."

"Not a problem," Willow said as she sent off the email.

Sturgeon

Willow was driving, so Travis could call the number he found on Mrs. Bayer's phone. Travis was also working the tablet, digging up past cases that might have the same MO. She turned on Cambridge and checked the houses. 1200 block. She needed 1415, so she drove ahead two blocks and began checking again, finding it right away. She pulled over and stopped in front of the light brown rambler.

There were two cars in the driveway and Travis did a quick search of the license plates and found they were registered to the gun owner at this address. The house was well kept up. The lawn was mowed. Flowers weren't blooming, but it was November, so. . .

They exited the cruiser. Willow walked around the cars on one side, and Travis the other, looking in and making sure they weren't occupied. They approached the door and Willow took the side closest to the yard. Travis, the garage side. Willow tried to glance between the slats in the windows, but there wasn't a clear view. Both detectives took up position away from the door and Travis rang the bell.

The door was answered after a few seconds by a woman who looked to be in her early eighties. Travis and

Willow both held up their badges and Travis introduced them, asking if she was Mrs. Bellamy.

"Cheese it! It's the cops!" she yelled back into the house. A man's hearty laugh came from the back and Willow saw him walk out of the kitchen area, holding part of a sandwich in one hand and a slice of cheese in the other. He brandished a smile.

"I'm Mrs. Bellamy, but if anyone did anything wrong, it's that old fart," she said to Travis, jerking her thumb over her shoulder.

"Hilarious, Sharon. Invite the officers in," the old fart admonished. Sharon stepped aside and opened the door fully. Travis walked in, followed by Willow.

"Are you William Bellamy?" Travis asked the man.

"Yes. What's happened? Are the children alright?"

"Oh. I'm sure, Mr. Bellamy. We're not here with bad news. Just seeking information."

"Well, what can I do for you, then?"

"Do you own a Garcia 380?" Travis asked.

"I used to. I bought it for the old hag, before she was an old hag. After trying for a year to teach her how to shoot, I gave up and sold it."

Sharon snatched the sandwich from him and took a bite, mumbling with her mouth full, "God, you're an irritating shit." She took the sandwich and went back to the kitchen.

The old fart watched her walk away and then turned back to the detectives with a smile. "A person could starve to death around here."

Stifling a laugh, Travis asked, "Do you know who you sold it to?"

"Yup. Naturally. Got a photocopy of his ID, as well." Bellamy walked toward the hallway and Travis followed. Willow stuck and kept an eye on the kitchen. After about three minutes, Travis came back out, thanking Mr. Bellamy.

"If something else comes up, we'll be in touch, Mr. Bellamy. Thanks for keeping records."

"No problem. Sometimes I wish I didn't. It would be nice if I had misplaced that marriage certificate."

"I heard that," came from the kitchen. "No sex for you, tonight."

Willow slapped her hand over her mouth and darted out the door before she lost it. Travis was on her heels. The two of them kept themselves together all the way to the cruiser and Willow quickly started it and drove away. They almost made it an entire block before they both burst out in tear-streaming laughter.

Willow watched Travis. He was laughing so hard he was shaking as he tried to enter the buyer's name into the tablet in the hopes of getting a current address without having to wait for research, which could take, at times, two or three hours, depending on how busy they were.

After a few blocks, they had both calmed down and Travis told her he had no luck with the tablet and had to email research. He continued to work with her on the intricacies of murder investigations, giving her the who-what-where-when-why speech, and the process they would go through to answer each 'w'.

"A lot of information can be gained in an assortment of ways," he said, "and I'll be having you with me on each interview with each employee, a Confidential Informant I have in the area, anything I ask research for, etcetera, etcetera."

"Good," Willow answered. "If there was anything I learned from that serial-killer case, it was how little I actually know. What's what with that number that was on the wife's phone?"

"It was a restaurant in Palo Alto. Not much help but we'll hold onto it for a bit. As far as our last case, you did fine, considering the shithead you had for a partner."

"Oh my God, I know. I was thinking that myself."

Travis laughed at the dig, "Let's head back to Historical Lane. I'll see what my CI knows before we start the interviews."

"So," Willow said, "they have six employees and they all have a key. Probably because of days off. According to Blankenship, she and this Max guy work Monday through Friday. She works mornings. He works in the afternoons and closes up. Which leaves Saturday mornings and fill-ins. It seems to me that any of them had access to the cash at any time. I doubt money was the motive."

"There you go assuming again, Will," Travis admonished. "You don't know that. Yes, it's possible that the robbery was an attempt to throw off investigators on the murder. It's also possible the murder was an attempt to cover up the robbery. To just outright steal the money would have got them arrested and jailed, but if the money was stolen with a killing, we're looking elsewhere. We will investigate all avenues."

"Yes sir, Detective First, sir," Willow quipped. "Can I see that badge again? It sure is pretty."

"No. It's mine and you can't see it."

"We're going to check to see who was in massive debt or needed drug money, right? That's property, and we can pawn that off on Billups and Fisher so we can focus on who had a beef with Bayer."

"Nope. It's all on us. You got some place to be?"

"Not at all. Gotcha. Do you have any preliminary thoughts?"

"None. Pull over here. I want to walk a bit. It's only two blocks from here, and I missed out yesterday on my exercise."

Willow did pull over and the two exited the cruiser and began walking down Historical Lane. She really had no idea who Travis' CI was, but she was sure she was about to find out. She couldn't wait to learn what questions he would ask the man. Or woman.

To her surprise he walked into the coffee shop across the street and just down from Arnold's. They walked up to the counter and he ordered a coffee, black. She ordered her usual green tea, and the two of them took a seat at a corner table. Before their drinks were even ready, a man walked in, waved at Travis and went to the counter himself. Once the man had his order placed, he walked up to their table and took an empty chair.

Birch

Travis introduced Greer Manfred. Manfred was the owner of the Antique store three shops down from Arnold's. He and Arnold met here each day for their morning coffee and local gossip. It was obvious Manfred was struggling with the death of a fellow shop owner and someone he called a friend.

"Have there been any rumblings around?" Travis asked. "Any unhappy customers? Workers?"

"I haven't heard a word. Whenever a conversation came up about Arnold, it was always preceded by 'What a nice guy'. I take it you're ruling out a random robbery?"

"Not at all," Travis answered. "It very well could have been, but we like to cover all avenues. Has there been any new competition open up lately?"

"No. The newest shop is that dress shop on Third, and it's been there for three years. I just can't believe this happened."

"How about this, Greer? Have you noticed anyone walking around the area in the past week or two? Maybe someone that's just window-shopping, but doing so more often than normal?"

"No. I would have immediately gone on alert and gone for a walk to each shop and warned them. Plus, I would have told Tina."

"I'm sorry," Willow interrupted. "Who's Tina?"

"Meter Maid," Travis answered. "But don't ever call her that. Greer, is there anyone else that you see on a daily basis besides Arnold, Tina and whatever that mail guy's name is?"

"Gracie, at lunch. I go there every day for my sandwich, and she would always have it ready for me. Geez, I wonder how she's handling this. She loved her job."

"Not well," Willow interjected, "but she seems strong. She'll be okay."

"Yeah," Greer acknowledged, and then looked down at his newly arrived coffee and clasped the cup in both hands. A moment of awkward silence followed as Manfred's eyes became moist with reflection.

"Greer," Travis said, drawing him back to the present. "Did Arnold have a partner, do you know? Did he say anything about anyone putting pressure on him?"

"No. It was just him. Like I said before, not a bad word from anyone."

"You're supposed to be making my job easier, Greer," Travis joked.

"Sorry," Manfred answered with a smile. "I will be keeping my eyes and ears open, though. This shouldn't have happened at all, much less to a guy like Arnold. I hope you catch the bastard."

"We're going to do everything we can. As usual, if you hear anything at all. Conversation, comments or anything at all, you call me."

"Oh yeah, I will."

Travis and Willow excused themselves and made their way out of the coffee shop, leaving the brooding Greer Manfred to his thoughts and memories. As they were walking out, they were stopped by one of the baristas. It was obvious Travis knew the girl, judging by the smile and his greeting.

"I hate to act selfish, Detective," she said, "but I open on weekdays. Am I safe?"

"I would appreciate it if you would stay alert to any potential danger, but I would say that at any time, Alicia. We will have units here more often than the norm, patrolling the street. You should be fine as long as you're alert."

"Thank you. That's not going to be a problem. I'm not getting out of my car if I see anyone I don't know."

"That's a good idea. Stay alert. Stay safe." Travis nodded a goodbye and he and Willow continued out the door.

"That was pretty uneventful," Willow said as they were walking to the car. "Not much help there. It tells me that It's looking less like a random act. Am I wrong again?"

"Not at all. In fact, you are one hundred percent correct. We can't rule it out, but it is looking less likely. Manfred is pretty alert. However, we also have the knowledge, now, that it is unlikely anyone in the area committed the murder. Arnold and Greer were pretty close. Arnold would have hinted at something to him."

"So. Our main focus should be on the employees, right?"

"That's where we'll start. Can you think of any other possibilities?"

"Obviously, the wife. What else?"

"Repairmen that he may have let in," Travis advised. "Vendors. Salesmen, and one other." Travis looked over at Willow and watched as the wheels turned. She was learning. Getting better every day. Less assuming. More digging. He waited. Just before they reached the car she came upon the epiphany.

"Manfred," she blurted.

"Yup," Travis said, patting her shoulder. "There was no break-in. The killer either had a key, was there all night, or had been let in by Arnold because he trusted them. It's a long list, and we need to get started. We'll head back to the station and start calling the employees. We'll talk to them first. I'll do the first one, and you'll do the rest. Pay attention to the questions I ask."

"Yes, sir. Detective First, sir." Willow smirked.

"Good. You know your place. I like that." Travis smiled, but Willow punched him anyway.

Willow drove, so Travis picked up the files and began looking for anything that would help them decide if one person stood out. He found nothing that jumped out at him, and decided the interviews would take place on a first-come, first-served basis.

After a few more minutes than usual, due to traffic, they did eventually reach the station. Travis wanted to stop in again at CSU. He wanted to know if the doc had found anything helpful, as well. He decided it would be more prudent to have Willow handle the crabby man while he was at CSU. The doc seemed to be more pleasant with new detectives. Probably because it was his chance to shine with suppositions.

As they entered, Willow turned to the coroner's office, and Travis into CSU, looking for Tara. Hopefully, he could avoid the other 'gentleman'. He looked back where he had last seen her, and it was apparently her duty station, because she was in the same place. She didn't seem to be working on the computer, but all three of her screens were spinning like crazy.

"Hi there," he greeted. "Remember me?"

"Of course. How are you, Detective?"

"Doing well. We're getting ready to get set up for interviews. How are you doing?"

"I'm making some progress. I sent you off an email about the 380. It is absolutely the murder weapon. Right now, the boys," she indicated her computer screens with her thumb, "are working on the tread of the boot prints, fingerprints near the busted glass, and those of the back door."

"Can I ask you, do you all work on the same cases, or do you each have specialties?"

"Murder cases have priority. If no one's available, then someone has to set their case aside until the murder case is done. We take cases in order, otherwise. We don't have specialties. Whoever's available handles the new case. If there is a murder, that tech becomes the boss, so to speak. Everyone works their own case, but if the murder tech needs help with something, their case goes on the back burner."

"Sounds complicated."

"Not really. We work pretty well together. Things go pretty smooth. That is unless the chief gets a wild hair up his nose, then it gets pretty frantic, like that serial rapist a couple years back. We all dropped everything and dove in.
We thought he was going to stroke out."

"Well, I don't want to keep you," Travis said. "It looks like you're working pretty fast, so I'll stop bothering you and wait for your emails. Thank you for your time."

"No problem. I'll get you things as fast as the searches allow," Tara said with a smile. She turned back into her cubby and notes.

Travis made his way upstairs to the V. Willow hadn't returned yet from the coroner, so he began reading the details of the report on the 380 from Tara.

Sturgeon

"Hey Doc. How goes it?" Willow asked, as she entered. Thankfully, she didn't see Jack anywhere. She was flattered by his attention but it could get sticky.

"I do the same thing all the time. How do you think it goes?"

"Aww, Doc. You love your job and you know it," Willow smiled out.

"There is absolutely nothing about this job to love. Everyone I deal with is dead."

"Yeah, I guess that would be hard to deal with. Sorry. On the bright side, though, you get to see our bright faces once in a while."

He stopped his work and looked over at her. He just shook his head and began telling her what she came in to find. "The victim was killed at close range by a bullet that entered his back three quarters of an inch to the left of his thoracic vertebrae. The bullet passed through the heart and lodged next to the third costae where it attaches to the sternum. I removed the bullet and sent it to the lab for analysis. Death was instantaneous.

"They are also in possession of his shirt," Fenowicz continued. "It had a residue that appeared similar to powder burns, and they are testing it against a weapon that was found at the scene. The rest of the wardrobe is there, as well, but there was nothing curious about those items, so it's probably not going to be a priority for them.

"Everything else you could want will be in the report that I'll email to you as soon as I finish. Which will be a lot sooner if a certain detective will vacate the room and let me do my job."

Willow smiled. "No one's ever going to call you Ducky, are they?"

Fenowicz just stared at her, looked at the door and then back at her. She took the hint and left the room, heading back upstairs. When she arrived, Travis was deep into his emails.

"I got nothing from the doc except that death was immediate and a lot of grumbling," she advised. "How about you?"

"The Garcia is our murder weapon but there were no prints. The tech is still working on the other prints, but I think all we're going to get are the prints from the employees. We'll need to print them all to eliminate them. Whatever is left will probably be the killer. It's unlikely there will be an unmatched set, though. He apparently wore gloves."

"I have a theory," Willow announced.

"That's nice," Travis responded. "Why don't you start setting up interviews? Be careful of your wording. These are interviews, not interrogations. Explain the need to eliminate their prints, etc. Once I get through here, we'll go visit the man Bellamy sold the 380 to."

Willow made sure Travis saw her frustration at not being able to share her theory but he didn't seem to care. He just looked at her with that 'get busy' expression and glanced pointedly from her to the phone. "I can do that while we're driving."

"Look, Will," Travis said compassionately, "I know you're eager to put this to bed but this is going to be a process. I have research working right now on whether this guy has reported any burglaries. He obviously no longer has the gun, so it was either stolen or he sold it. Or maybe, just maybe, he used it recently and tossed it in a dumpster. If he's our killer, he already has his story worked out. We need a conviction, not a theory."

"Fine," Willow said as she sat in her chair. She began sorting through the employee files and glanced over at Travis. She decided she would bring up Marci again. "Did you give your statement yet?"

Travis got that look he usually got when she asked a question he didn't want to answer. She really wanted to know what he thought but every time she asked, he would always dance around the subject.

"Hello?" she pressed.

"Yes, Willow. I gave my statement. This is not our decision and we should allow the process to unfold."

"In other words, you think she's going to lose her badge."

"I didn't say that," he snapped. "Quit speaking for me."

Willow wasn't going to let it go. Marci needed support. "Travis, I need to know. Did you say anything that's going to get her fired?"

"What I said is none of your business. We shouldn't even be talking about this. The board asked the questions and I answered every question truthfully. I offered nothing beyond my answers."

Willow could tell he was getting angry, but she pressed on. "I can tell by your tone. You do think she'll lose her badge."

Travis shrugged. Then, after a few uncomfortable seconds, he spoke, "There were six of us."

"He threw a two-hundred-pound police officer over the roof of his van," Willow blurted out. "She was afraid for her life."

Travis just shrugged again, paused and then repeated his previous statement, "There were six of us, Willow. She fired twice through the windshield. She wasn't even within reach of him. You took the behemoth out with your Taser. I know she's a friend. I know she's a nice gal. I know her record has been exemplary, but she fired twice at an unarmed man. It was unnecessary force. I'm sorry, Willow. I really am. But yes, I think she's going to be relieved of her badge. Now that I have said that, I'm also going to tell you it's not something I'm going to talk with you about any longer. Drop it."

"God!" Willow spouted, "That sucks!"

"I know. I'm sorry. Since we're back on the serial killer investigation, you should probably know I received an email from Thompson this morning. Sanders hung himself in his jail cell last night."

"Chulo got to him," Willow said. "That man really has connections."

"Yes, he does."

Willow was confused. "I thought Sanders was in protective custody."

"Wasn't much point," Travis explained. "The murder was put to bed, Sanders had no info to help with the Horace prosecution, and Chulo wasn't in custody. Prison seemed to be the safest option."

"Do you think it was a guard or one of the other inmates?"

"It was a guard. If not, he at least arranged it."

The conversation ebbed and Willow began calling the employees. It didn't help distract her from the realization that her friend Marci, currently on unpaid administrative leave, would never again don the blue or pin the badge. She had always known this would be the end result but she still held out hope that they would find some desk duty for her. Travis had just confirmed what Willow had feared. Then he attempted to take her mind off it by giving her something else to think about. Kind effort but futile.

Birch

Willow had finished setting up interviews, one of which would be this afternoon. Travis was certain they could check on the man Bellamy sold the gun to before they would have to be back for that interview. Two of the six employees had offered access to their homes for the interviews. Travis and Willow would only need to call first. One of those would be Blankenship, and that would be pretty quick since Willow had already interviewed her at the scene. With any luck they would be able to squeeze those two in today, too.

Andrew Carver was the man who'd bought the 380, and research had verified that he indeed had filed a burglary report two years ago. Research had sent Travis an email of the items listed as being taken, and the 380 was among them. That meant absolutely nothing, of course. It was possible there was no burglary at all and Carver just wanted to stick it to the insurance company.

Travis would take along the report and check to see if any of the missing items were in the house. He would have Willow study the report, as well. She could be a second set of eyes. He would also check with Davis. Davis was the officer that took the report. Officers usually could tell right away if it was an insurance scam or not. The property detectives would also need to be a priority.

Carver lived alone. Unusual for a man in his forties, but not unheard of. The address Travis was given was a middle-class neighborhood. Carver would need to have a fairly well-paying job to afford the place on his own. It could be he worked more than one job. Travis was confident he could break the man if he was indeed lying about the burglary.

"Let's hit the road, Will. I want to check this guy out and see if he has the same story he had when he filed the report. I'll drive. You can scan the report and help me check out his house and see if any of the reported missing items mysteriously reappeared."

"Are we going to call first and see if he's home?"

"Nope. If he doesn't answer the door, we'll check through the windows, back yard, sides. Since he was hit by a burglar, it's not out of the realm of possibilities that someone broke into his house and did him harm. We need to check."

Willow laughed. "That's not going to fly, and you know it."

"There's no need for it to fly. All we're doing is protecting and serving."

"And if we don't see anything?"

"Then we call the man and set up an appointment."

"Like nothing happened and we were never there?"

"That-a-girl."

"He's going to have neighbors, you know."

"That's fine. If they ask, we'll tell them. But only if they ask," Travis smirked. "Where are we going for lunch?"

"Your house."

"I'm making you lunch?"

"Nope. Kris is."

Dang it, Travis thought. Kris had texted him when he was talking with Manfred and he had forgot to call her back. She had left for work earlier than he had. He wondered what had happened to send her home early. It was unlikely she had been fired. Her bosses loved her, and with their financial situation, she certainly wouldn't have quit without another job lined up.

"Hmm," he said, "I wonder why she's home. She left before I did."

"Maybe if you had called her back earlier, you'd know," Willow offered.

Travis gave her a scowl. "You obviously do, so spill it."

"I don't think so. You shouldn't be blowing off your wife, and I don't like your attitude."

"My attitude? So, asking you to the dance is out, then, huh?"

They arrived at the Carver house and Travis parked at the curb. When they exited the car, Travis stepped up onto the sidewalk and pulled out his phone. Just as he opened the text to read his wife's words, Willow smiled and said, "She was forced to take two personal days or lose them."

Travis frowned at her and began to text a response with Willow looking over his shoulder.

[Sorry, Honey. Was in an interview and my train of thought. . .]

Willow poked him and pointed at the phone. "Change the word train to caboose."

"Okay, you know what . . .?" he began, but Willow was already approaching the house. He followed her and finished his text as he walked. When they reached the door, he stood on one side and Willow, the other. Travis rang the doorbell.

While they waited for Carver to answer the door, he and Willow both peeked in the windows to scan the living area for items on the list. Travis didn't notice anything, and he looked over at Willow but she just shrugged. After a proper amount of time passed, Travis knocked loudly.

That didn't work, either. Willow went one direction and Travis turned and went the other, and the two of them began taking advantage of every crease in the blinds to scan the interior of the home. After nearly ten minutes they met back at the front of the house.

"Anything?" Travis asked.

"Nothing that stands out. You?"

"Nada. Let's check the report and see where he works. If that fails, we'll call him and see if he can meet us somewhere."

"I think we should talk to the neighbors," Willow offered. "Maybe they know when he'll be home."

"The problem with that is police detectives are asking questions about him. Neighbors love to gossip. He may be totally innocent and we're putting him in a bad light."

"Yeah. I understand your thinking." With that, Willow turned and walked away. Away from the cruiser. Toward a neighbor's house.

"What did I just say?" Travis spouted.

"Hey," Willow responded, "I'm just following up on a burglary."

Travis growled to himself but turned the opposite direction to hit the neighbor on the other side. As he was walking up the driveway, he saw a woman weeding a garden on the side of her house. He pulled his ID.

"Good morning," he greeted. "I'm Detective Travis Birch, with CPD. Do you have a minute?"

"Sure," the woman answered. "What's up?"

"We're just following up on a burglary . . ."

"What?" the woman asked excitedly. "When did this happen?"

"It was actually a couple years ago but some new evidence has come to light and we were hoping to speak again with Mr. Carver. He doesn't seem to be home, however. Do you know when he's normally home?"

Travis noticed a look of disgust on the woman when he was asking and saw her shaking her head. She looked fairly young. Early to mid-twenties, maybe. She obviously knew nothing of the burglary and probably had moved in since then.

"We specifically asked that woman about crime when we moved in here. Obviously, realtors will tell you anything to sell the house."

Travis heard a baby crying and the woman pulled a monitor from her pocket and headed for the front door. "Andy usually gets home about the same time as my husband. Around four. I have to go. Thanks for sharing the burglary info." The woman continued toward the house, with a little more speed, obviously uncaring whether Travis was finished or not.

He looked across the street and saw an older gentleman watching him from the porch of the house directly across from Carver's. He moved in that direction.

Sturgeon

Willow walked up to the neighbor's door but before she could knock the door was opened by a man looking to be in his early fifties.

"Wow," he exclaimed. "Whatever it is you're selling, I'm sure I'm buying."

Willow pulled her badge and ID and showed it to the man, and his admiring eyes turned sheepish. "Detective Willow Sturgeon," she offered. "I appreciate the compliment." Then, with a half-smile, she continued, "You should have seen me a few months ago. I wonder if I might speak with you a moment about Mr. Carver's burglary."

"Absolutely. Please come in. Would you like some coffee or water?"

"Oh, no, thank you," Willow answered as she scanned the living room for items on Carver's list. "For the sake of our records, could I get your name?"

"Zack Albandian. Has there been a development? The other officer seemed pretty thorough."

"There has, and we're following up in the event someone remembers something they didn't mention to the officer. Were you contacted at all by detectives?"

"No, just the officer. He was good, though. I could tell he was interrogating me, but he did it in a professional manner."

"Why would he be interrogating you?"

"I don't know. Next-door neighbor, maybe. You know that burglary was committed by someone Andy knew, right?"

"There is a mention of it in the report, but why do you think so?"

"The items that were taken were the valuable things. A baseball card, a handgun. Things like that. No television or any electronics, actually. An antique vase. Other stuff that would probably raise questions at a pawn shop. Rare coins. Honestly, Andy was more upset about the baseball card than anything else."

"Why is that?"

"It was a 1952 Mickey Mantle rookie card in mint condition. Do you have any idea how much that is worth these days?"

"I didn't get that far in the report."

"50,000 easy. Maybe 60. Handed down from his dad."

"You know him pretty well then, right?"

"Yes, Detective. I do. We moved here about six months after Andy. We've known each other for fourteen years, and no, I have no problem taking a lie-detector test. I wouldn't steal from him."

"Let's not get ahead of ourselves, Mr. Albandian. I'm only asking because if you know him that well, you must know his acquaintances. Do you have an opinion on who might have done this?"

The man's casual look once again turned sheepish, and it was obvious to Willow he was not going to be forthcoming.

"The handgun was used in a murder, Mr. Albandian. This is not a time to be hesitant. You have an idea. I need to hear it."

Albandian cleared his throat and looked everywhere except at Willow, so she repeated herself, "Murder."

"Look, Detective. Andy is a friend of mine. If he finds out I said anything, that friendship is over."

"We know how to be discreet. Give me a name."

"Andy . . . Andy has a son. Andy got a woman pregnant in college. He wanted to marry her, but she refused. She wouldn't believe he loved her. She thought he was offering because of the pregnancy, and he couldn't convince her otherwise. The boy is in his early twenties now. He has no job, and from the sounds of it, never did."

"I'm listening. Nothing you've said so far shines my coins. What are you not telling me?"

"I met the young man once, when I was over at Andy's. It was just one of those cases where my instincts took over and told me to abandon ship. All the time we talked he had the 'cat that ate the canary' look about him. He was stand-offish and gave me the impression I didn't belong there. I thought maybe he was going to hit Andy up for money, so I left.

"In the conversations I've had with Andy since, I've learned that the boy has never asked him for money. The boy doesn't live with his mother, has no job, no disability. As far as I can tell, he has no source of income at all. How does he live?

"I can only think of three ways," Albandian offered. "Inheritance. Drug lord, or cat burglar."

"Entrepreneur," Willow offered. "His mom. Wealthy girlfriend. There are many ways."

"Andy would have mentioned those. The kid is bad news. He sent my hackles up."

"What's this boy's name?"

"Ken is his first name. I don't know which last name he goes by."

"Do you know the mother's name?"

"Hell yes. The only woman Andy ever talks about. Abigail Stockard. He still loves that woman. Probably why he never got married."

"Did she?"

"Never met her, and Andy never said."

"Okay. If we have any more questions, what number can we reach you at?" Willow wrote down the man's phone number, thanked him and exited the house.

She didn't see Travis anywhere, so she walked back to the cruiser and began perusing the Carver file again, looking for any mention of a son. She checked the reports of the officer and the detectives. There was no mention of a son. Both reports listed Carver as living alone.

Travis had the keys, so Willow didn't bother with the sync. She dialed the station and asked for Kramer.

"Kramer."

"Hey, Matt. It's Willow. We're out looking for info on a stolen gun and we're talking to the neighbors of the victim. Do you remember the Andrew Carver case?"

"Hmm. Oh, wait. That was the guy with the Mantle card, right?"

"That's the one. Do you remember any mention of Carver having a son?"

"Negative. His closest family member was in New Mexico. I remember that. Is that his son?"

"No. His son lives locally. I can't find mention of him in either report."

"He lied to us. Bring him in. I'll meet you at the jail."

"Calm down, Matt. There's more to the story. I'll brief you when we get in."

"To hell with that, Will. He lied in a police investigation. Where are you? I'll come to you."

"We're at 123, Matt-needs-to-take-a-pill Avenue. I'll talk to you later. Bubbye!"

"Damn it, Will . . ." Kramer was cut off as Willow disconnected. She began rereading each report, checking occasionally to see if Travis emerged. He eventually did, and when he looked her direction, she waved him over.

"What did you find?" he asked as he got in the car.

"We have another person of interest. Apparently, Mr. Carver has a son. A son he forgot to mention to the reporting officer or the guys."

"Well, don't tell Matt. He'll freak out. He hates liars."

"Too late. I think he's on his way here. I'm sure he got our location from dispatch."

Travis hesitated for a split second and then said, "You know what? I'm hungry. Let's go see Kris." He then started the engine and drove away from Carver's.

Ophidian

Ophidian took the name because of his ability to get out of tight spots. It was something he had always been able to do. He slithered his way in and slithered his way out. That was one thing that made him very popular. That and the fact that his services were paid for based on the person's wealth.

He had never turned down a reasonable job. That one man who wanted him to kill the president was a moron. Ophidian wasn't stupid. If the person he was sent to kill was too well protected, Ophidian would just tell the client to hire an army. Ophidian worked alone. Always. No one would ever know who he was for that very reason.

The income he made from his hobby was enough that he didn't need to work, but then if he didn't work, it would create questions and Ophidian couldn't allow questions. The pay was good, and on occasion the benefits were as well, depending on his client. The one thing he never did was a freebie. It was always one-third deposit for the honor of meeting him, and the balance when the job was done.

You would think that would cause a problem but it didn't. The client was never nervous about the one third, because they knew Ophidian always followed through. Ophidian was the one who had to fix the pay issues. There had been two occasions when the client didn't like the way the job was done and refused to pay. Ophidian's reputation was everything. The client knew he would do the job, and now they knew there were consequences to not paying.

He opened his refrigerator, pulled out his brown paper bag and opened it up for his inspection. Sandwich, apple, string cheese and package of cookies. He was set. Exiting out the back door, he sat on the picnic table that he had built. He always ate lunch at this table. He loved the outdoors. The umbrella provided the shade in the summer, but he hardly needed it this time of year. He raised his face to the sun and took a deep breath. Then he pulled out his sandwich.

The humdrum life of working inside a building made the time he had outside all that more enjoyable. Breathing the fresh air and admiring what leaves were left on the trees was pretty much the highlight of his day. It was closing on Thanksgiving and there weren't many leaves left, but those that were, were very colorful.

He smiled and waved at Walking Wanda, taking a bite of his sandwich. She smiled and waved back, continuing on her way. He had never met the woman, but he took lunch the same time every day and she walked the path behind his home at the same time every day, as well. Because this was a daily occurrence, he had given her the name after several waves and walks.

Thinking again of Thanksgiving, he was hoping it could just be him, his wife and their daughters. He was sick to death of her relatives inviting themselves to Holiday dinners because they were either too cheap or too lazy to cook their own. His family all lived in New Jersey, and they would never impose unless asked, anyway. He would have to remember to ask the wife if her family was coming.

If his wife had a little bit better understanding, it wouldn't be an issue. He would simply schedule his out-of-town excursions when his in-laws were in town. He had tried that once, though, and his wife had become cold for a couple of weeks.

When it came to his hobby, he preferred out-of-town gigs. The local police would always focus their investigations on local criminals. It became easy and less stressful not to have to worry about an alibi. He would slither into town and slither out after. Deed done. Payment received. Matter over.

However, it was not that simple when the job he was hired for was local. He would always need to make sure his bases were covered and he had all his ducks in a row before he executed his plan. He had to make sure he didn't use his own weapons and had his mask and gloves with him. He had to make sure he had an alibi, but mainly, an escape route was critical.

His most recent job had been, in fact, local. He had plenty of throw weapons, so he'd used one at the kill. At some point he would have to replenish his stock but for now he was still good. He had tossed the gun in a dumpster at the rear of the building, and had donned his too-large boots and left prints.

Ophidian had done his homework. He had been living here for quite some time. He read the papers, and studied public records and some that weren't. This was a pretty large city but it was severely lacking in police coverage. There weren't enough to cover the square miles of the city, but the real shortage came in the detective division.

He wasn't all that worried about that rookie but Birch was a challenge. He had stopped drinking. Ophidian remembered how Birch was before he took to the bottle. Birch had actually gotten pretty close, once. So close, in fact, that Ophidian had nearly packed up the family.

Then something happened. Ophidian couldn't ascertain what, but Birch began missing work. Ophidian followed him one day and Birch went right to a local bar and was there until closing. It was the best news Ophidian'd had in some time. Ophidian went months without taking a new job just to be sure. Birch kept up his routine so Ophidian went back to work.

Ophidian believed everyone on the planet wanted someone killed. Either someone from their past or someone from their present. It was a sad thing, and luckily most people would never act on it, but there it was. Those who did want to act on it hired Ophidian and others like him or simply did it themselves. Those too frightened to do it themselves were the ones who kept Ophidian in his toys. And he did love his toys. Lunch was over, so back to work he went.

Birch

Having each ignored phone calls from Kramer, Travis and Willow arrived at the house for lunch. Travis gave his wife a kiss and Willow gave her a hug. Travis knew there was no point trying to start a conversation with Kris, as today would be no different from any other day that Kris and Willow got together. Girl talk. He walked out the back door, sat at the patio table and called Kramer.

"What the hell, Travis? You guys screening your calls?"

"Yup. Only yours, though. Whenever someone else calls we answer."

"Where are you? Are you with that lying sack?"

"Nope, and you can drop it, now. This is a murder investigation. When we're done with him, I'll let you know."

"Bullshit. He lied to us."

"Someone lied to a police detective? Well, shit. Hang up. I'll call you back in a few minutes. I need to alert the media."

"Very funny."

"You need to get over this, Matt. People lie to the police all the time. You're going to stroke out one of these days."

"To Hell with you two. I'll ask Cap."

"Have fun." Travis and Kramer disconnected and Travis went back to thinking about the case. There was something about this case that smelled familiar but he couldn't put his finger on it. It had to be an employee, vendor or friend. Travis doubted the friend thing. Wouldn't he be visiting instead of adding receipts? Vendors require very little attention except to sign for a delivery. Killing Arnold in the back part of the store would have created less noise. That left employees. So why did he think it wasn't an employee?

Willow waved him in, and he took a seat at the table and told the two what he was thinking and what he surmised.

"First of all," Kris said, "why anyone would kill that sweet man is beyond me. He is always very kind."

"It's looking like a robbery," Willow added. "But when I talked to his day cashier, she was pretty adamant that Arnold would have given them the money without a second thought. This whole thing is mind-boggling."

"Maybe the killer didn't know that", Kris offered. "Maybe he was drugged up and just wanted to support his habit. I know you guys have a job to do, but if I can add my two cents, I don't think Arnold was killed by someone he knew. I agree with Travis. Arnold was the type of person, at least what I knew of him, who would rather visit than count. Even an employee or supplier."

Travis stayed silent during lunch and listened to Kris and Willow discuss the case back and forth across the table. He listened, absorbed, and stored their comments. In talking to each other and ignoring Travis, it was obvious neither his wife nor Willow thought the killer was known to Arnold. Travis wasn't sold yet, but they had valid views.

"Did you know Arnold provided free lunch one day to Stang Elementary when they took their field trip to Historical?" Kris asked, looking at Travis. Travis didn't respond, still running things through his head.

"Hellooo? Honey, are you even listening?" Kris asked, shaking Travis from his thoughts.

"Sorry, dear. Yes, I am. I have been absorbing everything, actually. I get the impression you both think this is a random act. It still doesn't explain how the killer got in. The doors were locked, according to that cashier who found him, and the killer didn't come in through the broken door."

Travis continued, "We have a few interviews this afternoon that may shed some light. I guess we'll see."

"Okay. Good luck. Both of you. By the way, we're taking the kids to Willow's. Pepper was the deciding factor."

"Okay," Travis said. "Sounds good. Let's get back to work, Pard."

On the way to the cruiser, Willow offered that Travis needed to get the kids a puppy and that all kids needed a puppy but before Travis could respond her phone rang. Her car was ready. She explained that she was at work and would pick it up after she got off.

"What time is our first interview?" Travis asked.

"Doesn't matter. We only need to call first. Everyone is currently unemployed."

"Okay," Travis responded. "Let's talk to them, see what they know, but I want to be back at Carver's by four. I'll drive. You call the two employees and check emails for anything from the doc, the lab or research."

As Travis was driving to the address of the employee, they would speak to first, several things went through his mind. None of which were the things Willow was working on. He thought she was right. Maybe it was time to get the kids a little cuddle-buddy. They were old enough now that they wouldn't accidentally hurt a puppy. He would have to do some research and see which breed would be best for kids.

He also wrestled with that nagging feeling that just wouldn't go away. There was something about this case. He just couldn't put his finger on it. There were no signature marks on the victim. There were no post-mortem stab wounds as there had been with the serial killer. There were no playing cards or any other like items. Something, though, something was there. He felt it more than he knew it. He made a mental note to spend as much time as he had available going over previous cases.

The thing that was really eating at him, though, was the text he had received from the captain during lunch, with specific instructions not to tell his partner until end of shift. Not being the one to tell his partner would have been wonderful. Now that he knew, though, he was having a feeling of betraying her by waiting.

"Willow. I'm afraid I have bad news," he blurted out before he lost his nerve. Willow looked over at him and he knew, right away, he didn't need to say more. He could tell by the onset of moisture in her eyes.

"Our union can kiss my ass," she spouted. "They should have been able to negotiate something. Desk duty. Holding cells. Something."

"She wouldn't be able to wear a badge, Will. Much less carry a gun."

Willow just shook her head and went back to the tablet. Travis continued on, looking over at her on occasion. He could tell that it was on her mind, but she continued to focus on the data. Travis already knew Willow was a hell of a friend, from his own experience, and he knew she would be on the phone to Marci at her first opportunity.

Sturgeon

Willow steeled herself, amidst the news she'd just received, as they were parking in front of the Blankenship house. She would stay professional and send an email off to the union in her off time. There was a murder to solve and she would help solve it. She would have to call Marci when she got off today.

"What plans do you have for Thanksgiving, other than us?" Travis asked, trying to take her mind off it. Nice of him to try.

"My brother won't fly in until Thursday afternoon, so mom is holding Turkey dinner until Friday. Saturday, we'll go to Adam and Jessie's, and Sunday to the Gaudiers'."

"That's a lot of turkey, Will. Are you going to be able to move next week?"

"It is a lot, Travis. It doesn't mean you have to eat it all," Willow responded with a smirk.

"Sacrilege! Thanksgiving is for stuffing."

"Not that kind of stuffing."

They arrived at the Blankenship house and were met at the front door by Gracie and a Chihuahua in

Gracie's arms. Willow officially introduced her to Travis and she reciprocated by introducing Willie.

"How are you, Grace?" Willow asked.

"I'm okay, I guess. You know. . ."

Travis jumped right in, "Ms. Blankenship. . ."

"Gracie," Gracie insisted.

"We are just following up with you to see if, maybe, since we last spoke, whether you might have remembered something, or seen something this morning."

"No. I'm sorry. I haven't really been thinking about it. I've been crying, mostly, and thinking about where I'll find a job."

"So, no cars driving away? Pedestrians? Strangers? Unusual cars in the area?"

"Just Jack. He's always sleeping, though."

"Who's Jack?" Travis prodded.

"He's our local homeless vet. He sleeps under the palm trees behind Antique Alley."

"Do you think he might have done this? Maybe needed a few bucks?"

That question earned Travis a snarl. "No! I don't. He's a veteran!" Gracie spouted in anger.

"I appreciate your respect for our veterans, Gracie. I really do. I'm not one, myself. I have had run-ins with them, though. They have done this country a great service, but they are still human and subject to human behavior."

"Define run-ins!" Gracie spouted, now staring daggers.

"Gracie," Willow interjected, "we're not trying to anger you. We have a murder to solve and we have to exhaust all possibilities."

"Jack is a sweetheart. He wouldn't hurt Arnold. We are where he got his meals. Yardell is where he got his blankets. Canary gave him a used tent. He tells us stories on our breaks. Get off of him."

"Gracie," Travis cut in, "how do you know for sure he's a real veteran?"

Gracie's eyes opened wide and her brow furrowed deep. "Oh. My. God. Get the hell out of my house."

"Gracie. . ." Willow started.

"GET. OUT."

Willow nudged Travis out the door. It appeared to her he wanted to continue but it would be fruitless, since they had somehow hit a touchy subject. She waited until they were nearly to the cruiser before speaking.

"That went well," she announced sarcastically.

"Yeah, we probably wouldn't have gotten much more cooperation out of her. I want to try to find this Jack guy. Are there any other employees between here and Historical?"

"One. A part-timer. Lisa Goldberg. She's one of the ones we only need to call first. I'll give her a buzz and see if she's home."

Travis took the wheel and began the drive toward Historical. Willow called Goldberg and she was indeed home. She worked the second shift at the children's hospital and worked weekends at Arnold's to supplement her income. Goldberg was a nurse's aide at the hospital and was hourly. She was a single mom, with a child of her own.

They arrived at the Goldberg apartment and were buzzed in by Lisa. Willow had taken the tablet from the cruiser and she checked her email for lab results and coroner info during the ride up to the third floor. She couldn't help but chuckle as she remembered the fit she had thrown when the tablet had been installed, and the comment from Mark about it being a good Frisbee.

Lisa answered the knock and invited them in. She was a proper host and offered them water or coffee, and both detectives accepted the water. Willow sat her tablet down and pulled out her notebook to jot down key words in the interview. Travis had said he was only going to do one and she would do the others. To her surprise, the first question he asked after the small talk wasn't about Arnold's popularity.

"Ms. Goldberg. Are you familiar with a man named Jack?" he asked.

"Soldier Jack? Hell yeah. He's hilarious and has some great stories. He parks it in the rear of Historical and will hit us up for a sandwich once in a while. Arnold told us to give him what he wants and write it off as spoilage. It's not every day. Maybe two or three times a week. Why?"

"We were talking to Ms. Blankenship about him and she became angry with us. I was just wondering if maybe you knew his background."

"Yeah. You probably should have come here first and I could have warned you. Gracie's grandpa was killed in Vietnam. She never knew him. She kind of took Jack in as her make-believe grandpa. She even offered him a room but he declined. He said it was a good way to ruin a relationship.
Jack is smart that way."

"Well, you won't throw things at us if we ask about him, will you?"

Lisa laughed. "I promise I won't."

"Did you notice any long conversations Arnold and Jack had? Maybe one that might have involved some elevated voices?"

"God. No. Jack's a sweetheart and Arnold is probably the best boss I've ever had. I've never heard him raise his voice. Of course, I work closing, so I don't really see that much of him."

"Who determined Jack was a veteran?"

"I'm sure it was Arnold. Why are we even talking about Jack? He didn't rob Arnold. He gets anything he wants. Why would he?"

"We're just covering our bases, Ms. Goldberg. It would seem Arnold was well-liked, and we would very much like to know who did this."

"As would I. That was a good job. He was a good man. I'm going to miss him."

"You said *was*. Do you have reason to believe the store won't re-open?"

"That would be nice, but it wouldn't be the same without Arnold, and who would run it?"

"Maybe his wife, or maybe she'll sell it and someone just as nice as Arnold will buy it. There are also other places in Historical looking for good help. I think the antique store on Third is hiring."

"I'm not working for that dick. He's ten years older than me and married but it didn't stop him from hitting on me. I guess because I'm a single mom, I must be hard up."

"Are we talking about Backyard Antiques?"

"Yup. Asked for my phone number, once. Asked me to dinner, another time. The third time I just asked him if he was going to buy something, before he asked something else."

"Who knew? I've run into him a time or two. Never got that vibe. Wasn't he a friend of Arnold's?"

"Couldn't tell ya. Like I said, I was the weekend closer and didn't see that much of Arnold. Saw way too much of the antique guy, though."

"I can understand that. Just a couple more questions. Did you notice anyone new hanging around Historical in the last couple of weeks? Or even in the store? Different cars in the lots? Anything out of the norm?"

"Not really. There was that guy that Tina was talking to last Saturday, but I think he was just trying to get out of a ticket," Lisa said, causing Travis to look at Willow. She took the hint and made a note to check parking tickets.

"Just one more thing," Travis continued. "Can you think of anyone who would want to hurt Arnold? Someone who may have had a beef with him?"

"No but if you find someone, I'll gladly kick their ass for you."

"Thank you very much for your time, Ms. Goldberg," Travis said, handing Lisa his card. "If you think of anything else, no matter how trivial, give us a call."

"I will do that."

Willow and Travis left the Goldberg apartment, making their way to the elevator. Willow wasn't sure if she should ask, but she was dying to know if Travis suspected his CI of such behavior. She decided not to. She did have another question, though.

"What's going on with you, Travis?"

"What do you mean?"

"For the last couple of hours, you've seemed distant. None of my business?"

"I don't know, Will. There's something about this case. I don't know what it is, but it's eating at me."

"Something familiar? We can create a couple of key words and let research's computers have fun."

"That's just it. I don't have any key words. I just can't put my finger on it. Let's get over and try to find Jack. Maybe he's in a box."

"Oh. That's hilarious. Don't go being all accusatory. Let's just feel him out."

"I don't need you to tell me my job, Will."

"Rowrrr."

Birch

When Travis and Willow arrived at Historical, Travis turned on First Street and made a left into the alley. He proceeded slowly, scanning his left as Willow scanned the right. After they had crossed Third, Willow tapped his shoulder and pointed at a man wearing a Vietnam hat and carrying a pack sack. Travis pulled the cruiser into a parking spot and he and Willow approached the man.

"How ya doin, sir?" Travis asked, showing his badge. "Can we have a minute of your time?"

The man opened his bag and took out an envelope and handed it to Travis.

"What's this?" Travis asked.

"That's my DD214, my birth certificate and my picture ID. That's why you're here, right? To verify I'm a real veteran?"

"It is one of the reasons." Travis handed him back the envelope without opening it. "It's not the main reason. We have a couple questions about Arnold's"

"I saw the police tape. What happened?"

"First of all, thank you for your service. Arnold's was robbed and Arnold himself was killed. We were hoping you might have been awake and heard a shot."

"I heard something, but I thought it was that car backfiring. That's really a shame. Arnold and those kids were good to me."

"They think pretty highly of you. Can I ask? Did you see the car?"

"I saw A car. About two or three minutes later. I was sleeping behind Burgess when I heard the pop. It naturally woke me up. That kind of noise always does. I walked to the edge and looked out at the street. A car drove by pretty slowly, doing the speed limit. Late model. Puke green. One guy inside."

"You're sure it was a guy?"

"Could have been a woman with a goatee." Jack kept his face stoic, but he was looking at Travis for an expression. Travis didn't provide one. He did notice his partner was stifling a laugh, though.

"Was there anything else you noticed besides the goatee? Did the man sit high in the car? Lower than normal?"

"About average. Had a hood on his sweatshirt. Car was not a compact, but not real large, either."

"What time was this?"

"Don't know. I don't have a watch. Still dark, though."

"How were you able to see this much if it was dark outside?"

"The car passed in front of Decker's. They always leave their lights on so the police can see inside. Lit the car up pretty good."

"Do you always sleep behind Burgess?"

"Almost always. They asked me to. They park their delivery vans behind the store. I keep an eye on them. They give me stuff and someone always brings me a donut and coffee when they get there."

"So, you're still providing a great service. Thank you, Jack. You've been very helpful," Travis said, handing Jack a business card. "If something else comes up, have someone call me and I'll meet you anywhere. Dinner is on us, today." Travis handed him a twenty and patted him on the shoulder, and he and Willow went back to the cruiser.

"Get that info out on a BOLO, right away," Travis said to Willow as he made his way to a waiting squad that had been watching the interview. "List it as wanted for questioning. We don't have enough for POI.

"Hey, how are you, Crocket?" Travis asked as he arrived. "You healing up okay?"

"I'm fine. You guys hear about Marcl?"

"Yeah. A shame. Will didn't take the news too well, but she'll be fine. Don't say anything to her about the legal battle going on between the union and the department. I don't want to get her hopes up."

"Come on, Birch. She's not a child. She'll find out."

"Maybe. What are you doing here?"

"My new area. It consists of Historical, Historical and . . . oh yeah. Historical."

"Seriously? That's your whole area?"

"Yup. The sarge wants maximum visibility to discourage future transgressions. If someone needs backup I can respond. Otherwise, I drive in circles."

"Sounds boring. We're looking for a light green midsized car with a driver having a goatee. Keep your eyes open for us. Thanks, Crocket."

Travis made his way back to the cruiser. He saw an older car drive up and park. It was Blankenship. She ran to Jack, put her hand on his arm and pointed at Travis. Probably asking if he was harassing Jack. Whatever Jack said satisfied her. She gave Travis a dirty look and ushered Jack into her front seat. Probably taking him for a meal.

Travis entered the cruiser, getting a smile from Willow. "I don't think she's going to be sending you a Christmas card, Travis."

"Dang it. I was looking forward to one." Travis looked at his phone. "3:15. Crocket has this area. Let's look around some of the residential streets on the way to Carver's for a light green car."

"That's not really much to go on, Travis."

"I know. Maybe we'll get lucky."

Sturgeon

Nothing materialized from their drive through assorted residential neighborhoods, and Willow hadn't expected anything. Now they sat in front of the Carver house, waiting for him to arrive. The neighbor had said he got home about the same time as her husband, and the husband had pulled into his garage about five minutes ago.

It was 4:15 now and there was still no sign of Carver. Of course, this wasn't a set appointment. Willow had wanted to call the man and set up a meeting but Travis nixed the idea, not wanting Carver to "prepare" for an interview. To Willow, it seemed like a waste of time to wait for a man who just as likely was throwing back a few with friends before coming home. She needed to learn, though, and she would study the ways and means of Travis Birch.

She nearly jumped out of her seat when Travis started screaming obscenities. He bolted from the cruiser heading to the rear. She looked in the side mirror and saw another cruiser. Kramer. She turned and saw an angered Travis with a look she had never seen on him before. He looked like he was about to start punching the man. Kramer appeared just as angry, and the two were screaming at each other. Willow exited to break up the verbal skirmish but stopped. Another car was coming from the opposite direction.

Carver pulled into his garage and she darted up the driveway with her best smile, hoping he wouldn't shut the garage door. He didn't. He exited his black pickup, returning her smile. Not only was he not driving a light green car, he was also not wearing a goatee. She pulled her badge.

"Mr. Carver?" she asked, for verification.

"Yes," he responded. "Has something happened?"

"We have had a development that is connected to your burglary two years ago. I was wondering if we might ask some follow-up questions."

"I don't know how much I'm going to remember, but I'll help with what I can. Please," he said, indicating the door leading to the house, "come inside. Would you like some coffee or tea?"

"Oh, no, thank you. We're fine." Willow followed Carver in and held the door open for the arriving Travis. Travis pushed the garage door button, closing the door.

"You okay, Partner?" Willow asked quietly. Travis, still showing a little scowl, just shook his head.

"You handle this. I need to calm down a bit. I'll pipe in if need be. Ask about the son as discreetly as possible."

Willow patted his shoulder and led the way, following Carver. Carver took a seat in a living room lounge chair, and Willow and Travis, not wanting to stand over him, took the couch.

"Mr. Carver, I'm Detective Sturgeon and this is Detective Birch. I'm afraid there's been a development related to the burglary you reported. The handgun stolen was used in a recent robbery and murder. We'd just like to ask you a few follow-up questions that might help us solve the crime."

"You've said that already, and like I said, I'm not sure I'm going to remember anything. You find the guy that sold my Mantle and you'll find the killer."

"We're working on that, Mr. Carver. In the meantime, how did the burglar gain entry?"

"He jimmied the bedroom window."

"Where did you keep the gun?"

"It was in my bedroom. In the bedside stand."

"And the Mantle card?"

"That was in a box on the top shelf, in my bedroom closet."

Willow needed to find a way to get Carver to allow Travis into the bedroom. She would need to make sure Carver wasn't suspicious about it, though.

"Have you repaired that window?"

"No. I touched up the paint, though."

"Was there anything else disturbed in the closet? Clothes? Other boxes?"

"Just one other box, but there wasn't anything in it but tax receipts. I guess it wasn't interesting."

"Did the two boxes look similar?"

"I don't think they did," Carver answered in a way that led Willow to believe someone else might, and that was the opening she needed.

"Do you still have the boxes?"

"I still do. Yes."

"Mr. Carver, I have just a few more questions. In the meantime, would it be okay with you if my partner took a look at that window and those boxes?"

"Have at it," Carver said, pointing toward the hallway. "Second door on the right."

Travis stood and walked toward the hallway, and Willow noticed a look on Carver's face, indicating to her he was having second thoughts about allowing Travis into his room. She jumped back in with the biggest shocker she could quickly come up with.

"Who else has keys to your house?"

"What? Why do you need to know that?"

"Mr. Carver. If you're going to start answering questions with questions this is going to get time consuming. Who else has keys to your house?"

"There's one hanging on a hook on the back patio."

"That's it? No relatives or trusted friends?"

"The family all live in Arizona."

"All of them? You have no family in town? Ex-wife? Children?"

"Never been married."

Willow looked up from her pad and leaned back on the couch. She made eye contact with Carver and didn't avert those eyes. Seconds passed before she spoke again.

"I'm going to ask this one more time, Mr. Carver. Do you have any family members in Carpel? Do you have any children living in this city?"

Willow could see that Carver knew he was had. He looked down, scratched his ear and let out a deep sigh. "I have a son through an ex-girlfriend. He's not involved."

"I'm glad you can say that with confidence, because I can tell from the original report, this was done by someone you know. Someone who's been in this house and knew where everything was. Your house wasn't trashed, Mr. Carver. No one took your television, your microwave or even your silverware. Who else has been in your house during that period?"

"He wouldn't steal from me. The Janssens spent time here for get-togethers. Zack is here once or twice a week, especially on Sundays, for beer and football. Friends from work, once in a while."

"Mr. Carver, let's move to the dining room," Willow said, pulling out a legal pad. "I want you to write down some names for me." She placed the pad on the table in front of him. "I also want you to make a little asterisk beside the name if you know for certain you showed them the Mantle card."

Willow needed to keep his mind on the pad and off Travis, who was taking way too long to check a window and a couple of boxes. "Try to remember phone numbers, addresses, how you know them and if they knew about the key in the back. Feel free to use the phone book in your cell as a guide.

"Also, indicate on the pad their relationship to you and phone numbers and addresses, as well as where they work. Does your son work?"

"Yeah. He's a graphic designer."

She was saved by the returning Travis, but she still needed to explain the time. "You forgot your tape measure again, didn't you?"

"Yeah, but I adapted. Used my cell phone. I'll measure it later." Willow sat at the table and Travis joined her. They exchanged looks, but otherwise left Carver to the quiet. It took nearly thirty minutes, but Carver finished the list.

"Mr. Carver, it's going to take us a bit to get to all these people," Willow announced, after Carver had finished. "I can't begin to tell you how unhappy I'm going to be if we find out you forewarned them. That's called impeding a murder investigation. If I stay happy, I'll talk to the former detectives about your little lie about your family. If not, you can kiss your job goodbye because you'll be residing elsewhere. Do you understand?"

Carver nodded. "Say you understand," Willow repeated.

"I understand."

"Have a nice day, Mr. Carver." With that, Willow and Travis exited the front door, making their way to the cruiser. "Anything interesting?" she asked Travis.

"The boxes are almost identical. The indentation in the window frame was made by a very thin screwdriver. There's no way the burglar came in through the window. The guys were right about that. It was someone who had access to Carver's house."

Travis got in the driver's seat and started the cruiser, but once again, just sat there staring at nothing. Willow knew he was trying to pinpoint whatever similarity this crime had with one in the past.

"I'm going to drop you off at the car dealer," he said. "I'll stop by the station and check a few things and make some notes. I'll see you at your place when we drop off the kids."

Willow just nodded but continued to watch Travis, hoping he could put it together.

Birch

Travis dropped off Willow at the car dealer and was now making his way to the station with his new ride-along, 'The Nag', as he had named it. That feeling of déjà vu.

He had already decided on his course of action. He couldn't exactly email the cases to his personal computer, so instead, he would load them on a thumb drive or two and take them home with him. He would then focus on cold cases and try to find similarities. For right now, he needed to stop thinking so hard about it and maybe it would come to him.

He cleared his mind and started admiring his surroundings as he drove. There wasn't much to admire. November brought along the ugliest trees in history. The only ones that were still in color were the palms, pines and a few fruit trees. The others had colorful leaves, but half on and half off. The city workers were continually blowing those leaves that had fallen.

He passed a residential street with a street sweeper working on the leaves that had fallen in the street. Citizens were working on their driveways and walkways. Some kids were walking home from their after-school activities, kicking leaves. November wasn't Travis' favorite month. Too much yardwork. Raking his own leaves. Covering Kris' plants. Cleaning out the gutters. *That-a-boy. Feel sorry for yourself. You're good at it.*

Who was he kidding? He wasn't going to be able to clear his mind of the case. Someone's life had been taken from them. Someone nice. Who knew what Arnold would have done in the future? He already supported a local kids' soccer team. What else could have been in store?

More annoyingly, he hadn't found anything helpful in Carver's bedroom. He had gone through a couple of drawers and lifted the mattress, checked the closet, including some pockets of the clothes hanging there, but he hadn't found the card. He wouldn't have been able to use it anyway. It would have been an illegal search, but it would have made him feel better. Had he found it; he would have just had to work on finding other evidence.

Carver wasn't the killer. Travis didn't know that for sure, but he felt it. He also felt Carver was associated in some way with the killer. That burglar had NOT come in through the window. He'd had a key, knew where the spare was or had used lock picks. If it was lock picks, that might also explain how he got into Arnold's.

Travis arrived at the station and, as usual, had to drive around a few minutes to find a parking spot. He entered through the side door and went, right away, to the lab, hoping to catch Tara still at her 'Boys'. She was.

"What time do you usually call it a day, Tara?" he asked.

"When I've done all that I can that day. What can I do for you, Detective?"

"I guess I don't know if you ever think along these lines but is there anything about what you're doing that reminds you of a previous case?"

"This kind of thing is always similar in most ways. Was there something in particular I should watch for?"

"I wish I knew. It's bugging me. Thanks, anyway. Go home."

"About another half hour. Have a good night."

Travis waved acknowledgement and left, noticing the lights off in the coroner's office. He proceeded upstairs. As soon as he got there, he was sorry he didn't visit with Tara longer.

"Hey, Birch," Kramer said, "I'm sorry I got out of hand. It won't happen again."

"I don't know what the deal is with you, Matt. You almost got to the point of interfering in a murder investigation."

"I know." Kramer lowered his head and studied his feet. "I'm sorry," he repeated, sticking out his hand. "Friends?"

Travis looked at the hand and wondered what this was all about. Then he understood.

"No," he said.

"No, what?"

"No, I'm not partnering you with Sturgeon when the captain leaves."

"Oh, come on, Birch. I've got seniority here."

"Yes, but you're more interested in personal attacks, like lying, than you are solving the case. I've already decided on Baggerly."

"Vice? You're shitting me, right? What the hell do they know about homicide?"

"He'll be fine. I've got things to do." He walked away from Kramer and to his desk and began looking through his drawers for his thumbs. He found the drives, sat in his chair and began the transfer.

He paged through the notes on the Carver interview that Willow had given him. He'd heard her words to Carver about forewarning the people on the list, and he believed Carver looked genuinely intimidated by her tone, but Travis knew the man would warn his son. That's what fathers do.

Travis made a note at the end of the pad to talk to Manfred. It was possible that he didn't think to mention homeless Jack because he saw him every day, but Travis was going to talk to his CI anyway. Just to make sure that he remembered not to leave anything out of his information in the future. Jack may yet become a key factor in solving this crime.

Travis made a note to himself to check the parking lot at Carver's work for a green car. He stuck the drives in his pocket and left the station. He remembered in time that he hadn't driven himself to work, so he went back to the desk and picked up the cruiser keys.

When he got home, he received a hug from the kids and a kiss from Kris. She headed off to the shower and he sat the kids at the kitchen table to do their homework, receiving a frown from each. While they were busy, he loaded the thumb drives onto his computer and opened the first file. A cold case murder from four years ago.

He went over every line of the report but found nothing that jogged his memory. It appeared the victim was a member of a local cartel, and there wasn't enough evidence for the DA to go to trial with it. He saw his own notes attached that indicated where the evidence pointed, but the POI's boys alibied him up. Liars!

He was about to open a second file when he felt eyes on him. He looked up and saw both kids no longer at the table. The eyes belonged to Kris, who stood at the door to his den with her arms folded across her chest. Fully dressed, with the kids sitting on the couch holding their jackets. Obviously, reviewing these cases was going to be time consuming.

"When I got out of the shower, I yelled out at you that I was done," Kris announced. "I guess you didn't hear me, huh!"

"Sorry, honey. Give me fifteen and I'll be ready." Travis sat the drives on his desk and raced past her, heading for the shower, the back of his neck burning from his wife's stare.

Sturgeon

Willow was a little frustrated. But she wasn't sure what she was frustrated about the most. She had tried three times to call Mark, and he wasn't answering. The only logical thing she could think of was that he was out in the field on a case, but still, he could have answered and just said he would call her back.

Then when she was on the treadmill, she had called Marci. Marci did answer and she was very depressed about losing her badge. Willow could understand that. There were people that would just move on with their life, and then there was Marci. Being a police officer was everything to her. Willow had done her best to console her friend and try not to let Marci detect how angry she was.

That call had lasted about fifteen minutes. She had hopped in the shower and then got everything ready for the arrival of the kids. Once she was all set for them, she picked up her phone again and called her union rep. He wasn't pleased to hear from her after hours, but he did explain the city's stance on Marci.

The conversation continued for another fifteen minutes, and with each passing minute, Willow found her voice elevating. It turned into a screaming match. Her rep basically told her to stay out of it, that it was a union matter, and that set her off. She wasn't all that thrilled to be told to mind her own business. Expletives were shared several times, and Willow eventually hung up on the man.

She saw Kris' car pull up, out front, so she took a deep breath and put on her best smile. Pepper ran to the front door and began dancing around. The kids burst through and immediately collapsed to the floor, getting their faces licked incessantly. Willow greeted Travis and Kris, accepted the kids' belongings, and invited them to sit, even knowing they would refuse. It was date night, and date night didn't include Willow. The two left, almost immediately, and Willow put the kids' toys in the reading room.

She walked back to the rolling and giggling scramble of bodies on the floor and asked if there was homework to do. She received two head-shakes. Willow crossed her arms and stood looking at the two for nearly a minute before they got the picture and stood to give her a hug and a "hi".

"Spaghetti, or grilled cheese sandwiches?" Willow asked.

"Spaghetti," came the simultaneous response.

Willow went to the kitchen and put the water on the stove, added the salt, and emptied the pasta sauce into a separate pan. Then she noticed three sets of eyes on her. Her first response was to Pepper. "What are you doing in the kitchen?" Pepper hung his head and backed out onto the carpeted hallway.

"I think I have this, guys," she said to the other two. "Was there something else I can help you with?"

"Can we watch SpongeBob?" Macy asked.

"Nice try. Mom already ratted you out before she left. You've reached your television limit for the week. You can play out back, or read, or if you want, you could clean the garage." Both of the kids darted out the back door like their pants were on fire. Willow went back to the dinner preparation. Her phone rang. It was Mark.

"Hi, honey," she answered.

"Hey, babe. Sorry I haven't answered. I've been having a bad day. How are you? How was work?"

"I'm good. I'm guessing my workday was better than yours. What's going on?"

"I don't want to talk about it. Maybe tomorrow. Don't really want to rehash and relive it again. The Department of Justice is here. They think the Chulo leak came from our team. They've been assholes all day. Maybe by tomorrow I'll be in the mood to give you a rundown."

"I have the kids for a few hours, but if you want to come over later, I'll bet I can make you feel better."

"As tempting as that sounds, I'm not good company right now. Can I have a rain check, though?"

"You will never need a raincheck, honey. The offer is an open one."

"See? Already, I feel better. I love you. I'll talk to you tomorrow, okay?"

"You'd better. I love you too."

Well that was certainly awful. Mark was her man. It was her job to help him through these kinds of days. She knew he would do the same for her. Now, she would be thinking all evening if there was more that she could have said to make him feel better.

The spaghetti was ready. She set the table and called the kids in. Surprisingly, neither one wanted milk, instead asking for water. After everyone washed up, they sat down to dinner. Willow asked about school. Both were happy to be out for Thanksgiving. They asked if she was coming over and she said she was, but they were disappointed to learn she wouldn't be bringing Pepper with her. She had apparently been curt in the conversation, because Macy asked if she was mad at them.

"No, sweetie. I'm just worried about someone. I'm sorry."

"Who are you worried about, Auntie? Is it Daddy?"

"No. It's Uncle Mark. Now eat your dinner before it gets cold."

"Where is he? How come he's not here?"

"He's at work," Willow responded, pointing at Macy's plate, letting her know the conversation was over.

When dinner was over, Macy helped Willow clean up. Ashton had better things to do. Specifically, playing with Pepper. Once the dishes were done and the table cleaned, Ashton and Macy each went to the reading room and picked out a book, and the three of them sat down to read.

Willow needed this reading time. She was suffering a whirlwind of emotion. Disappointment at not being with Mark in this tumultuous day in his life was eating at her. Relationships were supposed to be give-and-take, and she didn't feel she was giving all she could. She should be with him now. Helping him heal from his depressed state.

Mark was one of the few good things that happened to her while she was working that serial-killer case. When Travis was in rehab, the only way she could continue working the case was if she could partner up.

As it turned out, she got lucky in more ways than one. The FBI got involved in the case and Mark was the liaison assigned by Special Agent Lisa Tanner. He became her temporary partner and she was able to continue investigating.

She was unsure, at first. He was only supposed to be providing her with information from the agency. As it turned out, he helped with more than just his assignment. He was with her on every interview, and helped follow up on every lead. The more time she spent with him, the more she began to like him.

He was funny, charming, intelligent and witty. Finding faults in the man was difficult and it wasn't something she should be trying to do anyway. She wanted to get married and start a family. It had become obvious to her; she wasn't going to find a better man to start a family with. He was a keeper and she was going to keep him. All he needed to do was ask. Just pop that question.

He spent many nights at her house and she spent many at his. He had asked her to move in with him, which told her he felt the same about her. He already had the ring. She had found where he had hidden it. She just needed to be patient. The man was having trouble at work. He just wanted to be in the best frame of mind.

Willow was in love. She felt comfortable in his arms. Safe. Secure. She was going to do it. Moving in with him on a permanent basis was exactly what she wanted to do. They could worry about what to do with her house, another time.

Birch

Travis would always bring his work home. Always. Kris had to admit to herself, though, that he was excellent at masking it. Not this time, however. This time he was really out there. There was something about their case that was bothering him. At least, she assumed it was the case. Maybe it was Willow, or something totally different, but those topics he would usually discuss openly with her. Well, maybe not Willow. Because of the relationship she had with Willow, Travis might be reluctant in that regard. No. Kris was sure it was the case they were working on.

They were conversing during the drive to their dinner destination. It wasn't the ninety percent attention that she was accustomed to. He was answering her and responding appropriately but there was a hesitation in his speech. A small insignificant hesitation that no one but she would notice.

They were discussing a wide range of topics. The kids together. Individually. School and grades. Field trips. Electric bill. Her work. He was there but he wasn't. She reached over and put her hand on his shoulder. He reached up and patted it and smiled at her. She gave a light squeeze to see if she could feel any tightness in his muscles but he felt like Travis.

Kris was happier now. Much happier than that miserable two years when she and Travis were separated.

She didn't like the separation but there was nothing she could change about it. She absolutely could not subject her children to the turmoil caused by a constantly intoxicated father. Despite her best efforts to stay with him, she couldn't stop nagging him about his drinking. There were arguments. Loud arguments that caused the children to cry.

Then the intervention that was Willow Sturgeon happened. She had her husband back, now. The love of her life. The only man she had ever, or would ever, love.

Despite her love, she wasn't stupid. She was constantly on guard against drama or any setbacks that would cause him to relapse. She didn't hide things from him but she did 'manage' the conversations or bad news that came around. She had taken over the bills and dealt with school issues.

Willow had constantly cautioned her against "babying" him. Against changing things so much that he would notice and begin to feel unworthy of her. It was Willow's opinion that self-confidence was the key. Travis would be fine, she felt, as long as he had purpose.

Kris knew the kids helped, too. In fact, she questioned, humorously, whether she, herself, might be in the way. The man did have a rather healthy relationship with Ashton and Macy. They loved him equally. During the separation there was much conversation back and forth between the three of them about Daddy.

That was the past. She needed to stop dwelling on it and enjoy their reunion. She would still be cautious, but there was no need for anyone to know she was. She would just watch. Listen. Love and be loved. He loved her. A woman knows. Just like a man knows when the woman loves him. Talk is easy. Actions speak louder.

The conversation continued during the drive and she realized even the sound of his voice enlightened her. The strength behind it. The deep resonating sounds of his voice. It wasn't just the joy she felt hearing him speak. She could tell from his tone that he enjoyed speaking to her. It was, after all, as it should be. They were best friends.

"So, what made you change your mind and decide on McCallister's?" he asked, changing their current subject.

"If we're going to make this date night thing a tradition, I just figured we may as well do it right. Do you mind? I just think McCallister's is a little more romantic than Red Lobster. McCallister's has lobster and shrimp, too. In the event that's what I decide on, that is."

"I don't mind at all, sweetheart. If that's where you want to go, then that is where we go. I was just curious."

Kris gave another squeeze of the shoulder and smiled at him. Yes, she was cautious, but she was fearful, as well. Would she even survive if there were another separation? She was madly in love with this man. He was her life. Her happiness. Her security.

Even when they disagreed on something, it was calm and even sometimes hilarious, as they would exchange quips back and forth. The kids would even have fun taking sides, if the issue was about what to do on a particular day off. Sometimes, it would end with Travis and Ashton going to a monster-truck rally, while she and Macy went to a craft show.

That's what families do. They adapt. Kris knew they were a family again. She had every intention of becoming the glue that held it together. Give and take. It was all about give and take.

Travis pulled into the lot at McCallister's and parked. When they exited the car, the conversation continued to the front door. They were talking. They were a couple. Date night would bring back memories of their first dates and the effort Travis went through to gain her favor.

Her first impression during those times was a good one. A feeling came to her. She couldn't explain it if she had to, but she just knew, inside. He was the one. He still was.

Sturgeon

Willow had fun last night with the kids. The energy. The laughter. It had been an exhilarating evening. She loved the kids. They were always full of energy. Not just last night. Being able to spend time with children was the best therapy around. That had been the good part of the evening.

Her phone conversation with Marci? Not so much. Willow had tried to provide as much encouragement as possible, but it was obvious Marci wasn't going to be very upbeat anytime soon. She knew Marci had over-reacted but the woman loved her job and had no idea what she would do now.

Then there was the conversation with Mark, who just wasn't there. It was like she was talking to herself. His answers were very vague. Had she not been babysitting, she would have got in her car and driven over to his house. She was more than a little concerned about him. Her concern was going to have to wait until tonight, though. She had a job to do today.

Now she was backing out of her garage into a torrential downpour that was not unheard of this time of year. She had just gotten her car back from the shop and certainly hoped she didn't have to drive through any flooding.

She wasn't sure what Travis would have them doing today. Traipsing wet feet into someone's house wasn't going to work, and asking interviews to come to the station during a rainstorm wouldn't, either. Willow guessed they would be focusing on research until the rain let up.

The drive was entertaining, for sure. Rain in California always brought out the best in drivers. There was very little in the way of speeding but there were always a few interesting lane changes and a great deal of brake lights. She was fortunate to arrive at the station without too much puddle-jumping, and it only took her a few short minutes to find a parking space.

When she arrived at the V, Travis was already going through files. The entire detective division was packed. It looked like no one was on the road. Surprisingly, there wasn't much in the way of loafing, either. It looked like everyone was working at their desks. Then she realized that Travis was going to be the boss for a couple of weeks when the captain left for his vacation, and they were probably all trying to impress. The captain was the only one not in yet. "Good morning," she greeted.

"Hey, Will. We're going to be house-bound for a couple hours. Let's look up these names we got from Carver and see if any has a file."

"Okay. What are you working on there? Aren't the blue folders cold cases?"

"Yup. Just checking a few past cases to see if there's any similarities. Do you know Bobby Baggerly?"

"I've seen him around. I don't really know him. Why?"

"He's going to be your partner while the captain's gone. I'll introduce you in a few."

"Okay. Are we going to talk to Mrs. Bayer today?"

"That's not the plan. We'll save her for last." Travis pointed to the files. "Make sure you check what type of car they own and if their driver's license shows a goatee. Check the males first."

"Sure thing, boss," Willow said with a smile. Travis just gave her a raised eyebrow and a sneer.

When her computer was ready, she started with the name she was most interested in. Kenneth Andrew Stockard. She started with the driver's license and found that the son had a beard. It wasn't a full beard, but it wasn't a goatee, either. It might be confused for one in the dark, though. She studied everything about the license, including height, weight and expiration date, noted everything she could think of on her pad and moved on to registered vehicle.

Here we go. 2012 Hyundai Veloster. Green. Could they be this lucky? What would be his motive for killing Arnold, though? Willow stopped thinking of him as the killer as soon as she heard that little voice in her head that sounded an awful lot like Travis. *Stop jumping to conclusions.* That and the fact that Jack was pretty sure the car he saw wasn't a compact.

She continued to dig. Checking social networks. Doing internet searches. Looking up people on his friends list, trying to get an association with Arnold or his employees. She found nothing. It would be nice to get a warrant and check his banking history and phone records but they hardly had enough for the ADA to even allow them in his door.

She did a search on the Veloster to find out if it had a built-in trip GPS. She did a search on the most common phone providers to see if she could get his phone number and maybe track him that way. She sent an email off to research to see what they could find. They had more experience in digging than she did. Then she moved on to the next name.

She noticed Travis was still buried deep into cold cases. It was bugging her. "What is it you're looking for, Travis?"

"I have no idea. I wish I did."

"Why don't you give me a couple? Maybe I can help."

"You just keep on keeping on," he said, pointing at her desk. "I'll let you know if I need help."

Willow went back to her names and began digging on Albandian. Her phone dinged. It was a text from Amy.

[Can you pick me up at the airport tonight?]

[You bet. Flight# Time?]

[Southwest 241 6:40P]

[Meet you in baggage]

[Thx]

Willow went back to her digging and logging. She had been at it for nearly an hour. This was by far the most boring part of detective work. She looked out the window and saw the rain had stopped. What a great time it would be to stretch her legs and walk to the window and check the streets for puddling.

Before she stood, she noticed Travis was no longer paging through cold case files. He was now typing and seemed to have been for some time. Seeing him type made her realize she had been hearing the key strokes.

"Do you have something?"

"I do. Give me a minute. I'm sending off emails to research."

Willow hoped that meant they could get away from these desks and actually get out and do some foot-work. Anything other than sitting on her butt would work for her. She went to the window on the pretense of getting a cup of coffee. Travis knew she didn't drink that mud, but no one else did.

Looking out the window and picking up a Styrofoam cup, she saw the streets were wet, but clear. Time to hit the bricks. She went back to the desk, looked at the cup in her hands and tossed it into the trash. Travis had stopped typing and was organizing the files.

"Will," he started, "I need you to put every name we have on this case onto a typed document and print it. Print it twice, just in case we lose one. I'm going to run down to evidence and check on something."

"What did you find?"

"An old case from a couple years back. Unsolved. The killer broke into the house using a window jimmy. He or she then killed the man. When they left, they broke the window to make it look like a home invasion. I remember the case. The victim was a partner in a landscaping business. I seem to remember thinking it was a hit. I'll be right back."

Willow began typing out every name they had, whether they were suspect or not. When she finished, she printed the document and went to the printer. There was already a document there, with names. Probably initiated by Travis. The case was from 2016 so she grabbed all the pages and went back to the desk and began comparing names.

There were no matches. Two had the same surname, but Samuels was hardly anything to go on. She didn't think that mattered to Travis. There was a reason he wanted the list made, and she didn't think comparison was the reason. Her phone rang. It was Travis.

"Yes?"

"Hey, Will. I forgot to mention this. While I'm in evidence, I want you to take a copy of the list of names, along with the one already on the printer, down to Social.

Tell Pete you want a deep search. Make sure he understands deep. Emphasize the word."

"You want him to search the deep web. Got it."

"Geez, Willow," Travis screeched in her ear. "Did anyone hear you say that?"

"No. No one's around me. Why?"

"We're the police. We don't do the dark web. Do not use the word web. Just tell him you want a deep search. He'll take it from there."

"Got it. On my way."

"Thanks."

Travis disconnected. Willow made a copy of both lists and made her way to the stairs. Walking into Social, she pulled the door a little to mask her voice. Then she handed Pete the two documents.

"What's this, Willow?" he asked, eying the semi closed door.

"Pete, when you're not sending things out to the public, can you do a search on these names? A deep search?"

Pete was looking at the lists, but when Willow used the word deep, he looked up at her, so she knew he'd understood. Willow had always considered Pete a computer geek, and he even looked the part. Eyeglasses. Too-short pants. The whole works, actually.

"Criminy, Willow. Do you have any idea how long each of these names is going to take to load?"

"It takes as long as it takes, Pete. We're homicide investigators looking into what may be a murder for hire. We'll appreciate any help you come up with."

"Fine. Now listen. I will call you with anything I find. Tell shithead not to be calling me every ten minutes."

"Shithead? Do I get to call him that, too?"

"Please do."

Willow left Pete to his fun and went back to the V. Travis had still not returned so she decided to do a quick check of the coffee pot. The streets were only mildly damp. Time to get out of this confinement and out to the streets. She began organizing her desk and putting the files together.

Birch

Travis noted a difference in Willow, this morning. She was masking it and, in all likelihood, no one else was going to notice. Travis did, though. She was his partner and his friend. He knew it had something to do with Marci. He was certain Willow had taken the first opportunity she had after work, yesterday, to call her friend. Willow was a caring woman.

He signed into evidence, and while the officer was retrieving the lot number he'd requested, Travis wondered if this wasn't a job Marci could hold. Evidence officers didn't carry a gun. At least he had never seen one carry. It didn't mean they weren't assigned. Maybe the officer never donned it because he didn't see the need. Travis would check with HR. If they weren't required, he would let Willow know for when she spoke to the union, which he knew she would.

He received the box and sat at the table, sifting through every piece. There was nothing helpful. Not one piece of the evidence before him was even remotely similar to his current case. He was going to have to rely on the file. The witness statements. The first-responder reports. The CSU and Morgue reports. This case was linked, somehow. He just had to find out how.

He handed the box back to the officer, waited for him to verify the contents, and watched as the officer initialed the return-to-evidence voucher. Travis took the voucher and began the climb back to the detective bureau.

Instead of returning to the V, he entered the captain's office and closed the door.

"What's up, Birch? You closed the door. Does that mean Sturgeon is on your case again?" the captain asked.

"No. She's doing well. Do you remember the Hanford case? About two years ago? The disguised entry?"

"No. Refresh me."

"We never caught the guy. It's unsolved. Now we have another case with what may be a disguised entry. The killer entered by some means, either a key or lock pick, and then jimmied the window to make the officers and myself think he came in through the window. He also broke a window pane in the front of the house. That made it look like a home invasion in an effort to cover the bedroom window entrance.

"However," Travis continued, "he didn't come through the bedroom window, either. He either had a key, or lock picks."

"Now I remember," the captain said. "Either of those two options would have created mud, leaves or grass inside. It had rained. The floors were clean. As I recall, you were pretty adamant that picks had been used, not a key."

"Why? Do you remember?"

"Nope. That was the time your bender started and you were missing time. You never said."

"I know. I can't remember why I thought that, but I do remember being positively sure."

"Check with Miller. Maybe you said something to him."

"I'll give that a try. Thanks, Cap."

Travis left the captain's office and proceeded to the V. Miller wasn't around, so Travis sent him off an email, asking if he had any memories of the Hanford case. Travis watched Willow fidgeting. He smiled and shook his head. "You really don't do inside very well, do you?"

"Nope. Hate it. Always have. Always will."

"Okay. Before we head out, I want you to think about something. I have a pretty strong feeling that we are looking at a murder for hire. I want you to think about how we go about finding out who would benefit from Arnold's death. As we progress through the day, you can share your thoughts."

"The wife," Willow responded.

"Why?"

"Oh. We need a why?"

"Hilarious. Pack it up. I'll be done in a few. Did you contact Pete?"

"Yup. I sure did, shithead."

Travis laughed. "Yeah. He gets a little annoyed at me. You did correct him, right? It's shithead first-grade now."

"No. I forgot. Can I see that badge again?"

"Nope. Is everything okay, Will? You seem a little preoccupied."

"I'm fine," Willow responded. "Mark was a little weird last night is all. Strange phone call."

"Probably had a bad day at work. I know you guys have this thing about personal business at work, so maybe stop over after work and ask. Don't bottle."

"I can't tonight. I have to pick Amy up at the airport, and you know them. I won't be able to just drop her off and then leave."

Travis did know. The Gaudiers were kind almost to a fault and Willow was right. They would not understand that she wouldn't stay for dinner. He wondered momentarily if Willow had alerted everyone that she wouldn't be home tonight, for them to partake in her exercise equipment. It was only momentarily, however. He remembered catching part of her conversation with Kris at lunch. Kris was going to sub for her tonight.

He finished his emails and gathered his gear. With Willow in tow, he exited the building and went to the cruiser. "I want to pop over and see Jack, first. We'll show him a picture of that car and the photo of the guy and see if he can definitely rule him out. Hopefully, Gracie hasn't hid the man from us."

"He doesn't seem the type to hide," Willow responded.

"I agree. I'll drive. Why don't you send an email off to research and see if they can find out if Arnold had an insurance policy with a recent upgrade."

There were still a few clouds around but it was obvious to Travis that they were through with the rain today. The darker clouds were moving off to the east. They should be able to talk to a lot of people today. "What do we have for interviews?"

"Max," Willow responded, "and all the other employees, as well. I set them all up an hour apart. If we run over on one, I'll call and let the others know. A few on the list that Carver gave us, I can do by phone. I already did a lot of digging on most of them and I don't think they're going to pan out, but there are a couple that we're probably going to want to talk to face to face."

Travis nodded acknowledgement and then paid attention to the drive. He did notice, and hear, Willow not waste any time in calling the aforementioned persons. Her questions were sharp and gave the person on the other end an opportunity to slip up with info she hadn't mentioned. She was going to be good at the job. Getting better by the day.

When he arrived at Historical, he saw Crocket's unit but didn't see Crocket. Travis guessed him to be stretching his legs along the strip and just, generally, being seen. Travis drove to the rear alley and slowly moved along, looking for Jack. He found him when he crossed Third, sitting on a bench, having coffee with Gracie.

Jack saw the cruiser and waved. Gracie scowled and pulled Jack's hand back down. Travis was going to have to make amends with Gracie or she would become a problem shutting Jack up. He pulled the cruiser to a stop and parked in a nearby parking spot. Willow was still interviewing, but did point at Travis and smile.

He stepped out of the cruiser and approached the bench. Gracie stood and put herself between Jack and Travis. "Leave him alone."

"Stop it, Gracie," Jack intervened. "He's just doing his job."

"Ms. Blankenship," Travis greeted, "Jack is not a suspect. He is a witness. A very valuable one. I have some pictures I want him to look at. If that's okay with you, that is."

Jack laughed. Gracie scowled deeper but did move aside, and Travis continued to approach the bench. Gracie parked herself between Jack and her dog, Willie, so Travis had to stand. He opened the file and handed the two pictures to Jack.

"Could this have been the car, Jack? I know it was dark and far away, but that person and that car are of interest in this case."

"No, on the car. It was bigger than that. If you can picture a car bigger than this but smaller than yours, you'll be on track. As far as the guy, I can't say for sure. He was inside the car. I don't remember there being this much of a beard, either."

"Jack, you saw who killed Arnold?" Gracie wanted to know.

"I don't know that for sure, Gracie. I may have heard a gunshot and seen a car drive away. It's his job to know if I saw who killed Arnold," Jack answered, pointing at Travis.

Travis thought maybe Jack had just softened Gracie up a bit, but when she followed his finger, the scowl returned instead.

"Have you thought of anything else that may help us find the guy?" Travis asked.

"Not that I can think of. I have been re-working that morning in my head, but I've come up empty. Ideas *and* my head," Jack said, with a smile. Gracie squeezed his arm, not appreciating the humor.

"You still have my number, and you'll call if you remember anything, right?"

"I do and I will."

"Thank you, Jack," Travis said. "Ms. Blankenship," he added. Jack smiled. Gracie frowned. Travis turned and walked back to the cruiser. He had really gotten on

Gracie's bad side, but he knew there wasn't a future relationship there, anyway, so he shrugged it off.

Maxwell

Mark was beside himself. The DOJ was all over this place and his turn in the "Green Room" was next. He had no idea what these interviews were about. The agents that had gone in before him all looked like they had just come through a haunted house. They had been at it for two days, now. This being the second.

Homeland Security had been in and out. The DEA. Even a couple of the people from the Attorney General's office had made an appearance. No one who had already been interviewed was allowed to talk when they came out, so he was ignorant of the topic. To make matters worse, He hadn't seen Lisa all day. He didn't know if she had even checked in yet.

He had tried pinging her phone but the GPS was apparently turned off, which was a big policy violation for the FBI. He tried her unit and found it. It was still at her house. He tried her house phone but that went directly to voicemail. He had left a message but hadn't received a call back. He was uneasy about the current happenings. Something was going on, and it irked him that he didn't know what.

He had to find a way to have someone check on Lisa. He had a very uneasy feeling that something had happened. Maybe something did. Were these interviews about her? Had something happened to her and the DOJ thought one of her team had done it?

Stephanie and Carlos had already been interviewed but they wouldn't even get out the gate until the DOJ was satisfied. Willow had her own case she was trying to solve.

He would have to wait until it was his turn to find out. He couldn't possibly be the only one that had noticed her absence.

"Agent Maxwell," the man's voice boomed across the room. His turn. He stood and walked toward the man speaking. When he reached the man, he received a smile and a handshake.

"Jonathan Stark, Department of Justice. How are you today?"

"I'll be a lot better when I know what's going on," Mark answered.

"Have a seat. We'll fill you in as we go. Would you like some coffee? Water?"

"Tacos would be nice. I haven't had lunch yet," Mark said as he took the empty chair. He guessed from scanning the occupants that only two were DOJ. The other two, he wasn't sure.

"Fresh out. I'll bet we can find a donut, though," Stark said with a smile.

"Pass. I'm good. What can I do for you?"

"An admission of guilt would be nice. I'm eager to have this done with. I was enjoying a nice game of solitaire when this came up."

"Maybe I can oblige. What's the crime?"

"Oh, man. There are so many. We'll provide you with a printout you can sign when we're done here."

Mark looked at the man, smiled, and sat back with his hands clasped behind his head.

"Charles Logan," Stark offered.

"What about him?"

"How long have you known him?" Stark asked.

"Never met the man," Mark answered. Mark felt he was being set up for something. Either that or this was a chicken shit tactic from the early twentieth century. Charles Logan, also known as Chulo, had eluded the DEA in that massive late-summer sting in Charmaine. The DEA had the man dead to rights, but someone had tipped him off and he'd escaped. It appeared the DOJ was looking at Mark or some other member of his team as the tipster.

"That's not what we heard, Agent," one of the others piped in. "Our source tells us the sting was outed by your team. Specifically, you."

"Your source is leaking oil. I never met the man. You're leaking oil, too. If you were so sure I'm your man, I would have been the first one in here. How about you stop talking to me like I'm in grammar school and slap the cuffs on. After that circus act you just put on, I'm about to walk out. I've got work to do."

"Oh, you have time," Stark said. "Your work station is currently occupied."

Mark looked through the windows and saw a young female at his station. She was probably digging through his emails. Another woman, who looked even younger, was walking toward them. She entered the green room and walked up to him.

"Hand over your phone to the nice lady, Agent," Stark said.

Mark pulled his phone from his pocket and handed it to her, but she didn't take it. She said nothing, but he knew she was waiting for him to unlock it. He did, and this time she took it, walking out of the room. He noticed all the other agents were lined up against the wall and all their stations were likewise occupied. Why would that be necessary if they thought he was the mole?

"Detective Willow Olivia Sturgeon," Stark spouted.

Mark cocked his head. "Be careful, now, Jonny boy. She's my girlfriend, about to be my fiancée, and hopefully within a year my wife. You might want to tread lightly."

"My grandma used to call me that. You're not my grandma," Stark said.

"Don't be so sure. I could be. This interview resembles the twilight zone, after all."

"She was a key figure in the Logan investigation, right?"

"Wrong. That was a Charmaine operation. She's Carpel," Mark responded. "And since everyone connected to that case is dead, except Chulo, his girls, and his righthand man, Horace, my guess would be that Horace is your source. Not very reliable."

Mark continued, "None of Chulo's girls knew any names of anybody involved in the investigation, so it couldn't be them. It can't be Sanders, because he conveniently hung himself in his cell. We all know he didn't hang himself. Chulo arranged it. He had people inside the prison. The same prison Horace is in.

"Your source," Mark continued, "is flawed. You're all flawed. Every one of you. You come in here half-cocked, with information that is questionable at best. You halt our investigations and interrupt our stations without a shred of proof, and every single one of you has missed the most important detail in your detail-disoriented interviews."

It had dawned on him, suddenly. He wasn't sure at what point of the interview, but it did pop into his head. Nothing had happened to Lisa. She had been awfully quick to put an end to that serial killer. Not because she wanted to get back to the domestic terrorists. It was because the killer knew about Chulo. Mark's boss was the mole.

He paused, looked around the room at each of them, and then asked his question, "Where the hell is Special Agent Tanner?"

"That's not your concern, Agent. You have enough to worry about," Stark answered. "Is it your intention to cast blame on the Special Agent?"

"Casting blame without proof is your job. I'm just asking a question. Have you interviewed her yet? Why isn't she here, speaking for her team?"

"Do you need someone to speak for you?" asked one of the others, a man who looked more like a college nerd than a DOJ agent.

"I don't know, do I?" Mark responded and then stared the man down. "Are you guys the best the DOJ has to offer? Because you're really botching this operation."

"Oh, please instruct us on the proper manner," Stark said sarcastically.

"Should I? Where's my rep? If you are so certain your source is reliable, why wasn't I read my rights? Your first step should have been seeing to it I had an attorney present. You're fishing and you suck at it. Let me know when you have something concrete." Mark stood and walked out, making his way over to his fellow agents lining the wall.

Sturgeon

Willow checked her phone again. For about the tenth time today. Still no word from Mark. No call. No text. No nothing. She wasn't the paranoid type and told herself to stay calm. If Mark was breaking up with her, he would have said something by now. He wasn't the shy type and was brutally honest. Travis was returning to the cruiser, so she went back to the files.

"Any luck?" she asked as he entered the cruiser.

"Nah. The picture of that car wasn't a hit. He said it was too small. Let's go talk to the son anyway. Then I want to go see the wife."

"Let's do it," Willow responded, setting the files aside and buckling her belt.

She should have spent a couple of minutes and called Mark. Too late, now. She didn't want to call him in front of Travis, just in case.

Her interviews over the phone had not been very helpful, other than eliminating several that had been out of town at the tIme, and providing her with good information for her to verify. Travis had turned onto Max's street and was searching house numbers, so she put the files down and helped him.

They found Max's house and parked in front. Willow picked up the file pertaining to Arnold's murder, and the two of them exited the cruiser and walked up the approach.

"You're handling this," Travis said, reiterating his earlier comments about the interviews. If she forgot to ask a question, he would intercede, but otherwise it was her baby.

"Got it," she acknowledged, ringing the doorbell. The door was opened right away by a man who looked to be in his early twenties.

"Max Ringold?" she asked.

He answered to the positive, so she introduced herself and Travis and they were let into the house, offered the usual refreshments, which they declined, and then ushered to his living room.

Alibi. "Mr. Ringold," Willow began, "as I explained, we'll take up as little of your time as possible. Can you tell me when you first learned of Mr. Bayer's death?"

"Gracie called me yesterday morning. Woke me up. At first, I thought I was having a nightmare."

"What time was that, do you remember?"

"I think it was before nine. She was crying, and sounded frightened. She said she and Matilda were backed into a corner, waiting for the police."

"When you closed up, the night before, did you notice anything strange? Unusual vehicles in the area, anyone standing around?"

"No. I don't pay that much attention. I probably should have. By that time, I'm usually thinking about what to do for the rest of the night. Did you talk to Soldier Jack?"

"We did. He wasn't by the store. You said you were thinking of what to do for the rest of the night. Did you find anything? Any idea what time you got to sleep?"

Max smiled, knowing he was being asked for an alibi. "She left about one A.M. I was in bed and asleep by one-oh five."

"Who's she?" Willow asked.

"Caitlyn Hampshire. My girlfriend. I didn't kill Arnold, Detective, and neither did she."

Relationship. "No one is saying you did, Mr. Ringold. There has been a murder, and we will stop at nothing to find the killer. Nothing. Can you give me the phone number of Ms. Hampshire, so I can verify that?"

Max provided the number and Willow continued, "By eliminating all of the possibilities, we will be left with probabilities. What was your relationship with Arnold Bayer like?"

"There really wasn't one, other than he was the boss. He was usually gone a couple of hours into my shift."

"Was he a good boss?"

"He never had a bad word to say about any of the employees, so yeah. For my part, he was a great boss."

Willow noticed that Travis was giving the impression he wasn't paying attention, but she knew better. He was just scanning the interior of the room. He was looking for items on Carver's report or anything else that might help.

"So, as far as you know, no one had a beef with Arnold?" she continued.

"I can't imagine anyone. He seemed to get along with everyone. Especially his customers."

"He never mentioned having trouble at home, or with friends?"

"Not to me."

"Were there any new vendors at the store? Repairmen? Anyone out of the normal daily routine?"

"You'll have to ask Gracie about that. Vendors aren't, or weren't, allowed, except on Gracie's shift. As far as repairmen, the refrigeration guy came in to fix the upright a couple months back. Otherwise, I never saw one."

"Can you think of any reason, regardless of severity, that anyone would want to hurt Arnold?"

"God, no. He was a really nice guy. They didn't have to kill him. He would have given them the money. He professed that to us all the time."

Willow started to stir, as if she was about to leave. A trick Travis had taught her. "Oh. One more thing, Mr. Ringold. Do you own a gun?"

"Nope. Never saw a need."

"Well, thank you for your time, Mr. Ringold." Willow extended her best smile. "Did this go like you thought it would? If you were investigating Arnold's death, what question would you have asked?"

"Hmm, I don't know. Maybe I would have asked if you knew who killed Arnold."

"Do you? What does your human instinct tell you? Who do you suspect? If you knew for a fact that one of his employees killed him, who would be the first one you would go after?"

"Are you kidding me? One of the guys did this?"

"We don't know that. We're just playing a game here. Play along."

"I'm going to lose this game. I have no clue."

Willow nodded and held Max's eyes for an extra second or two, then she turned to Travis. "You ready, partner? You didn't nod off, did you?"

"Nope," Travis responded. "Let's hit the road."

As they left the house, having thanked Max, Willow glanced at Travis to see if he looked displeased but she couldn't see it.

"So. How'd I do?" she asked.

"You did fine. I think we're barking up the wrong tree, though. I don't think any of these employees killed Arnold. There's a lot of respect there. Let's change course. Call the wife. See if she's home. Let's rule out people he knew."

Willow did. Mrs. Bayer didn't answer but that didn't necessarily mean she wasn't home. It could be that she didn't feel like talking and didn't recognize the number. Willow said as much to Travis. As she suspected, they were going to go to the house anyway. Just in case. Willow's mind, once again, returned to Mark as well as Marci's termination.

Ophidian

Ophidian had been wrong about the rookie detective. Her questions were sharp. Distinct. She had also asked the same question twice. She had reworded it the second time, but it was the same question. He had pretended not to notice and just provided the same answer.

Now Ophidian had to make a decision. Moving his family was not going to work for him. He had changed his thinking about that option. Instead of moving to flee the threat, he was simply going to have to eliminate the threat. He hadn't received the last portion of the payment, so it wasn't like his client was long for this world, anyway. He would need to eliminate the only person who could link him to the job.

He was now in his garage. His trunk was open and he was assembling his long-range. The Glock case was also there and was opened as well. He wasn't taking any chances, and had added his pistol grip pump to his arsenal. In reality, he was probably only going to need the Glock, but Ophidian was nothing if not prepared.

With everything set, he loaded the Glock, attached his silencer, and closed the trunk. He kept everything in the trunk, in case he was stopped by a local squad. He slid into the driver's seat, opened the garage door and pulled out onto the driveway, closing the garage.

He entered the address into his phone and set it to start. Cautiously, as always, he pulled out onto the road and began following the GPS lady's directions. He had no intention of taking any action during daylight hours, but if the opportunity presented itself, he would. What he would probably end up doing was drive by her house, survey the area, see if he could notice any signs of security alarms or neighborhood watches, and return after dark.

Keeping his speed at 1 mph below the speed limit, with the help of his cruise control, Ophidian followed the directions given him by his GPS. According to her, it would take a short twenty minutes to get there. It was his intention to drive the area and try to find his best place to perch himself and take the shot. That option not being available, he would find a place to park in order to gain access to her house while she was sleeping. His third option would be to lie in wait for her to leave the house and follow her to her destination, and do her there.

The time was fairly accurate, and he was disappointed to find option one already eliminated. The house was one in the company of many in a decade-old residential area. There were no water towers, electrical substations, or corner markets for him to climb and set his scope. He continued to drive the area anyway, planning his escape route, should something go awry. It became necessary for him to wave at two joggers on two different streets. Not doing so might cause them to do a double-take on his car.

He came to a stop sign. Unusual for California residential streets but convenient nonetheless. It was the cross street he was looking for. There was no one behind him, so he sat there and looked right, then left. To the left, about six houses down on the right, a man and a woman were standing at a door. The woman was the rookie detective that had questioned him, and the man was Birch. The rookie was knocking on the door and Birch was trying to peer in the door-side window. Ophidian did another check in his rear-view mirror. There was still no one behind him, so he continued to watch the duo. Birch, it seemed from his vantage point, had lost a good deal of weight.

The rookie wasn't getting an answer, so she knocked again. Then she looked his way, poking Birch and pointing at Ophidian. Shit. He was just sitting at the intersection. What had alerted her? He acted nonchalant and proceeded through, slowly, with his head facing forward, but his eyes on them. They were both darting for the street. He gunned it and tore through the streets, heading for the main road. What the hell? Did he have 'see me' painted on his car, or what?

He had chosen this time on purpose. There was no way they could single him out during lunch hour, and he seriously doubted that if it came to it, they would put people in danger with a car chase. He kept checking his mirror until he reached the main road. Just as he turned on the road, he noticed them swinging around a corner, trying to catch up. He sped up, darting in and out for a few short seconds, then pulled in front of a box van, reducing his speed to match.

Behind him the light had turned red, so they would have to stop and wait for traffic to clear before they could pull out. He would be a full two stoplights ahead by the time they did. He kept his eyes open for traffic lights. If he could catch a left turn light in the green, he would take it. Otherwise, he would take a right when he came to a red light.

Something had tipped her off. She was too far away to notice his face, so he could only assume it was his car. The thing was paid off anyway. Maybe it was time to get a different ride. It wasn't like he couldn't afford one. Wait. Could she have noticed the goatee? Surely, not from that distance. Maybe. It was time to change things up. He'd shave that, too. Just to be safe.

There was no doubt about one thing. He had been seen. There was a witness. He was going to have to step up the pace and find out who the witness was. He was also going to have to give Birch and the rook something else to think about, besides him. The light turned red to his front, so he swung over to the right lane and turned off the road.

He was in a commercial area with a lot of larger trucks, and he took advantage of every one of them. He kept checking his rear view. There was no sign of the detectives. He had lost them. He turned left on the road that would take him all the way to his street and drove the speed limit the entire distance. The patrol units that Birch would have called would be looking the other direction. The direction he had originally gone.

He pulled into his garage and closed the door behind him, opening his trunk. He now had two witnesses he had to get rid of. The client and the witness who had seen him, whoever that might be. The weapons would probably be different for each of them. He walked to and unlocked the back door out of the garage, and unlocked his "tool" shed.

His wife wouldn't be home for another hour. He began, slowly and methodically, removing everything from his vehicle. His weapons went into the hidden panel in his tool shed. Everything else he just sat atop his work bench. He was going to have to do an internet search on the most common make and color of cars currently on Northern California roads. It was going to have to be a passenger car. The most common was probably some SUV or van but he couldn't have a vehicle that allowed his weapons to be seen from outside. He needed a car with a trunk. Preferably a used model five or six years old.

When his wife got home, he would take her car to Historical and strike up a few conversations. There were going to be plenty of people eager to talk about the robbery and murder. It should be pretty easy to find out who the witness was. He didn't think his client would be all that willing to admit her involvement. He would eliminate the witness first, and then her.

Birch

There had been no conversation in the cruiser for the last five minutes. Travis was incensed that the man had eluded him, and Willow recognized it. A man with a goatee driving a green car in a residential area occupied by the victim's wife? Travis didn't believe in coincidences. He had a pretty good grasp on things, now. He was certain goatee man had been hired by Mrs. Bayer. Goatee-man was probably there to collect his due. One way or the other.

Mrs. Bayer was obviously not home. Willow had knocked twice before she'd noticed the green car sitting at the stop sign. The woman was probably out trying to decide what she was going to do with the insurance money. Travis was going to have to make sure she didn't collect.

"I don't suppose you got any part of the plate," he asked.

"No. We were never close enough."

Travis pulled over into a corner parking lot, put the cruiser into park, shut off the engine and stepped out. He began pacing back and forth along the driver's side of the vehicle. Willow stayed seated but watched the pacing.

He had to find a way to get the Bayer woman's cell phone. He needed to get into her house to do a search. Maybe she had a computer. Maybe she had access to the dark web. Maybe she had notes lying around. Maybe. Maybe. Maybe.

There had been no communication from any of the squads that had been alerted of the green car. The guy was gone. Time for a new tactic. He re-entered the cruiser, started the engine, buckled up and exited the lot.

"Where to now, Travis?" Willow asked.

"We're going to see Miranda."

"Who's Miranda?"

"The ADA," Travis responded.

"You're on a first-name basis with the ADA?"

"There's no one there named Miranda. That's just what we call them."

Willow hesitated a moment and then stated the obvious, "We have nothing that would interest them. You know that, right?"

"It doesn't hurt to try. Besides, it will make them think about the case. Sometimes, if I can find Vicki, she has some ideas that help. The rest of them are looking for giftwrapping. Eliminating reasonable doubt is our key. You and I. However, with the ADAs, they all ask for zero doubt. They never get it but if they ask, eliminating reasonable doubt won't be so hard to obtain. The question we're going to be asked, right away, is do we have probable cause, and if we say yes, they're going to want us to elaborate."

"Probable cause for what, Travis?"

"I think the guy in the green car was there to kill Mrs. Bayer. Why else would he expose himself to her? We need to get into that house and do a search. We also need to search her phone, computer or anything else she has that may have helped her connect to the guy. We're also going to talk to Miranda about what we can offer as incentive. Provided, that is, that the threat of him killing her doesn't do the trick."

"There's something else to think about," Willow added. "Jack."

"Explain."

"The way he took off, goatee-guy knew he was made. Either the car or the recognition of his face. In his mind, we would have been too far away for the face to be an issue, so he would think someone must have seen the car at the crime scene. Not only have we seen that car for the last time, but he's also going to try to find out who saw it."

Willow was right. The man had bolted as soon as he saw her point at him. He would dump the car. Not at a car dealer, though. He'd trash it somewhere and buy a new one from a private seller. They don't care who buys the car as long as they get their money. Would the insurance company care who bought his car, or what had happened to it? Travis wasn't sure.

"Send a notice out to the squads to watch for green cars at used car lots. It was a Chevy so any lot is suspect.

Then call your insurance company and ask them if you got rid of your car, would they care how. When you finish that, call Blankenship and tell her what you think is possible. Have her pick Jack up and take him to her house until we can get there."

Travis was now even more upset that the man had eluded them. He had deliberately fled. It wasn't just an innocent person driving to work. He was their guy. Now they needed to find a way to re-locate him.

There was nothing noticeable on the car to indicate where the man worked, and Travis hadn't noticed a hat. The man had sped off so fast that neither Travis nor Willow had time to snap a photo for a more detailed look. They essentially had nothing. They really needed to break Mrs. Bayer. Since Arnold was a store owner, Travis was sure an attorney was going to jump in somewhere. He needed to break her before she saw a need.

Willow was now talking to her insurance agent. The squad memo must have gone out already. He was still five minutes away from the ADA's office, so he made a detour. He could stop at Blankenship's house without veering off course more than a couple of minutes.

Willow finished her call and he stopped in front of Blankenship's at the same time. He asked Willow to check if she could house Jack for a short time. In the meantime, he dialed research.

"Research, this is Mary."

"Mary, Detective Birch. Do you have a way to check for life insurance policies?"

"We do. I'll need a name of the deceased and company. We put a hold on the payment until we get the proper court orders to obtain the info."

"What if I don't know the company?"

"It'll add three and a half years to the search."

"Come on, Mary. Seriously, can it be done?"

"Yeah, but it will take a while. It depends on the person we speak to at the assorted companies. Sometimes they can be real dicks."

"Okay. The man's name is Arnold Bayer. It's the Historical murder case. Let me know if you find the company, and stop payment if you can. I'll try for the warrants."

"Will do."

"Thanks, Mary. I owe ya."

"A fifty-dollar gift card at Olive Garden should cover it."

"I'll see what I can do," Travis responded. He hung up with research and saw Willow back on her phone, texting someone. He also saw Blankenship backing out of her garage as she was getting back in the cruiser.

"She's willing?" he asked Willow.

"She's going to get him now. Guess what?"

"She thinks I'm the greatest man ever?" Travis guessed.

"No. No, Travis. That is so far from the correct guess. Mark's boss was the mole."

Bergen

FBI Special Agent Lisa Tanner was almost at the border. She was on I-5, passing Bellingham, and it wouldn't be that much longer before she was back in the arms of her man. This had been a horrible few months for her. As secure as she was in her own company, she was surprised at how lonely she had become without Chulo. A couple more hours.

She had taken care of business. She had left all the items that the FBI could use to track her back at her house. She had given herself the head start she needed by encouraging Horace to implicate Maxwell as the mole. She had packed the few things she wanted to keep into her suitcase, and changed cars. Her new ride was as plain as could be. A three-year-old Camry.

Her name had changed. She was now Mikayla Bergen. She had her passport and all the papers she would need. Her false work record, school history. She had even placed a traffic ticket on her record.

Women didn't need to get a face lift. They could do it themselves. She changed her hair color. She gave herself an extra cup size. She changed her makeup, giving herself a deeper tan. She now looked like a sun-tanned Detective Sturgeon.

She had placed a couple of bits of classified info in the file of Charles (Chulo) Logan, suspecting him of relocating in Mexico. She had even provided a fake witness seeing him drive away in a Ford pickup.

It was time for a change, anyway. When she had first applied at the FBI, she was the routine gung-ho recruit. She worked hard, every day. She studied. She worked out. She aced all the courses and became an agent. She had loved the FBI. She was somebody. Over the years, however, the bureau became more and more political. It just wasn't fun anymore. Washington, DC, wasn't the only place housing corrupt politicians. The FBI had their own, now.

Between her and Chulo, there was enough money that neither would have to work again. A few intelligently placed Canadian investments would assure it, and if there was one thing that Chulo, now known as Wilson, was good at, it was seeing the future.

She would call him in a few minutes. She was getting hungry, so decided to stop at Ferndale for a bite. She would call him from there.

She did her routine look to the sky for any high-flying helicopters and saw none. Even though she knew she had covered her bases well, she continued to be alert to possible tails. There had been a couple of cars following her several times on the trip, matching her speed, but when she took a turn-off, they had kept driving.

Wilson was going to meet her in Vancouver, where they would stay the night. Then, in the morning, they would both move on to Calgary and their new home. Lisa—no, Mikayla—was looking forward to being a part-time housewife, part-time worker. No more pressure to locate terrorist cells, no more politics. A nice, relaxed housewife. Wilson had not yet popped the question, but she really wasn't too worried about it. Even if he never did, it would be okay with her, as long as she had him.

She was approaching the Ferndale exit. The two cars that had been following should continue on. Ferndale was not exactly Seattle. The odds of two cars taking the exit were slim. She turned off, and both cars did indeed continue on. She found a Subway right away, pulled in and went inside. There were no other customers except her. Perfect. It wasn't dinner time yet, anyway, so the crowd wouldn't come until she was gone.

Mikayla watched them build her sandwich, poured her drink and sat at a table. She pulled out her burner to call Wilson, but then put it back in her purse. Another car had pulled up in front. Not just any car, one of the ones that hadn't exited with her. Same Nevada plates.

The man walked in, smiled and nodded. She returned the gesture but focused again on her sandwich, listening to him order. She watched, without staring, as he moved along the preparation line, having them add his ingredients. He paid for his sandwich, chips and drink and took a table behind her. She continued to eat her meal.

Her drink was low, so she stood, walked to the drink machine and re-filled her cup.

When she returned to her table, she took a different chair. This time, facing him. She pulled her sandwich over and looked at the man, sizing him up. He was definitely Government. She had been found, somehow. She reworked things in her head, trying to decide where she had gone wrong. They probably had known for some time and were waiting for her to lead them to Wilson. In which case this idiot blew the operation.

She stared at the man while eating. He looked at her and smiled again but this time she didn't return the smile. "Is it just you?" she asked.

"I'm sorry?" he responded with a fake-confused look.

"Is it just you, or are we waiting for a female agent? You're not very good at your job. You need to be trained all over again. You screwed up a covert operation. You'll probably be fired. I'll not lead you to him. You only have me, now. Is that good enough?"

The man's smile slowly disappeared and was replaced by a look of disgust. "Are you thinking I'm going to need help, Special Agent?"

"You need help, alright. Like I said. Re-training is in your near future. I'm assuming we're waiting for a female agent, because you're not frisking me. I'll kick your ass."

The two employees behind the counter, having been listening, had quickly disappeared into the back. There was no need. She had no intention of adding murder of a federal agent to her crime, although it certainly would be easy enough with this doofus.

"I can call one if you like. I'm not sure this needs to turn violent," the man said.

"The alternative is you handcuff me without a search. Make a decision. At least act like you know what you're doing," Mikayla responded, finishing her last bite and leaning back in her chair.

The man dialed his phone, and when it was answered, he spoke, "Sir, this is Agent Dalton. I need a female agent at the Ferndale exit Subway. Yes, sir. I thought I could get a feel for her if I got up close." The man pulled the phone slightly from his ear and Mikayla smirked.

"Maybe you'd be lucky if they re-trained you," she said, laughing.

"Yes, sir," the man said again into the phone. He repeated the two words two more times, and then hung up.

"Was he being mean?" Mikayla asked with a pouting expression. The man wasn't enjoying the humor. She wasn't either, really. It would be simple to overpower this guy, but she had been found out, and evading the DOJ now was out of the question.

She had blown it. She had lost Wilson. There was no way he would take a chance on visiting her in prison, and she knew that even if by some miracle she was released, or her attorney worked some magic, she could never go to him. They would follow her. They already knew he was in Canada. Thumping this imbecile was suddenly looking like a good idea. She knew it would do no good. She still couldn't go to Wilson.

Birch

"He told you that? I thought all that stuff was supposed to be confidential," Travis asked, responding to Willow's statement about Lisa Tanner.

"I'll get the full story tonight. He's going to try to get out early enough to come with me to pick up Amy. All I got was 'S.A.L.T. is the mole. More later'. I called him and told him about Amy and he said he would meet me at home."

"Some of that investigation is making sense, now. She must have planted those vials I found."

"Yeah, and she was too quick to have the guy killed. He knew about Chulo."

The two of them rode the rest of the way to the ADA in silence, both wrapped up in their own thoughts about that hectic last few hours of the serial-killer case, and FBI Special Agent Lisa Tanner's involvement.

When they arrived at the ADA's office, Travis explained that it wasn't a two-person job to schmooze the ADA into agreeing to obtain a warrant. He wanted Willow to spend the time on the files, emails, phone interviews, and staying in touch with Blankenship, making sure she had Jack. He also wanted her to check in on research about Bayer's life insurance, the coroner, and to call Pete and have him also look for possible hitmen while he was deep.

Travis exited the cruiser and climbed the stairs to the offices, working over in his head what he would say. The first thing he was going to do was look for Vicki. If she was free, he was definitely going to be speaking with her. Even when she denied him, she was helpful with her suggestions. The other knuckleheads just said no and they were busy, so beat it.

He took the elevator up and exited on her floor, going right away to her office. He looked through her window, and for once, she was not on the phone, instead having her head buried in her computer. He opened the door.

"Well, hello, Detective. What brings you to my stoop?" Vicki said as she indicated an empty chair.

"I'm going to try to save a life. Maybe more than one. And I need some help," Travis responded.

"Let's hear it."

"Two days ago, a man was killed in Historical. It was made to look like a robbery, but it wasn't. We . . ."

"How do you know?" Vicki interrupted.

"Routine investigation showed there were attempts made to distract us from the real evidence, such as a disguised entry. The victim showed no signs of being aware of any noise. The real entry was made with a key, and quietly," Travis said in a half-truth.

"We interviewed all the employees," he continued, "and we're confident they're not involved. The only other person that would have had a key is the wife. We don't think she killed her husband, but we do think she hired a man to kill him.

"Today, we went to her house," Travis continued, "and while we were there, a suspect and vehicle showed up that matched a witness description. We think he was there to kill her, eliminating someone that could tie him to the murder. Unfortunately, he eluded us in a high-speed chase."

"Let me stop you right there, Detective," Vicki said. "First of all, what do you want from me? Because that will determine my questions and my statements."

"A safe house for my witness, first of all," Travis responded. "A search warrant to get into the house of the victim would be nice, as well."

Vicki just sat and stared at him, leaning back in her chair, with her chin resting on her cupped hand and a single finger stretched along her mouth. She was thinking. He knew that. She was trying to decide what the judge would say when she went for the warrant.

"Why won't the wife let you into the house? Does she know you suspect her?"

"That's unlikely. We haven't even talked to her since we delivered the news." Travis knew what the next question was going to be. Vicki would want to know if the wife had looked distraught when the news was delivered.

"Did it look to be a shock to her? I don't understand why she wouldn't want to find her husband's killer."

"You know as well as I do that there are a lot of really good actors out there that Hollywood hasn't found yet. My partner has been relentless talking to the employees. The wife is the only other person with a key. It's possible that she will be cooperative, but it's also possible that she won't."

"What would be her motive, detective? Does she have money troubles? Is there another man? Did he have a gazillion-dollar life-insurance policy?"

"I'll let you know as soon as I get the warrant," Travis said with a smile.

"This isn't a chicken-versus-egg debate, Detective," Vicki said without a smile. "I am the one who has to face a judge and tell him Detective Birch has 'a feeling in his gut'."

Travis knew he was asking a lot from her. He knew he didn't have a set motive. Regardless of evidence or suspicion, he knew he didn't have much to stand on unless he had an answer to the 'why' question. "I know she had him killed. I know her life is in danger because of it. I know my witness' life is in danger. This is not a down-on-his-luck cowboy who just needed the money. This is a killing machine that is practiced at it and very deceptive. Tell me what you need from me to help me save them both."

"That's just it. You don't know. You are very good at your job. I know that. But you always mistake your thoughts for fact. I need facts. Hard evidence. I don't want her to die any more than you do but the system is the system. I'll get you a safe house for your witness. I'll get you a court order that will compel the wife to speak with you. I will not attempt to get a judge to give you the right to tear her house apart until you get me that hard evidence. A reason why she would want him dead. Evidence of a communication between her and a known hitman. A recent change in the victim's insurance policy. Communication between her and someone wanting to buy the victim's business. Witnesses. Evidence. A reason she would benefit from his death. Smoking gun kind of stuff."

"Understood," Travis responded, running both hands along his scalp.

"I'll have someone call you when I have the place set up and security in place. What did this witness see?"

"He heard the gunshots and saw the car drive away and described the driver."

"Weak, but I'll give it a try. I'm sorry I wasn't more help."

"You've been very helpful. As usual. I appreciate it. Thanks for your time." Travis stood and walked out. He hadn't gotten everything he wanted, but he seldom did. The next step would be keeping Jack safe.

Soldier Jack

The coffee shop had provided Jack with an expired sandwich and a cup of coffee, so he was sitting back by the dumpsters enjoying his lunch. He pulled out the paperback book he had found and began reading the blurb on the back cover. He was happy to see it was a series of short stories. Perfect.

He opened to the first page but didn't even get a sentence read before the honk. Gracie. What in the world was Gracie doing here? He waved and she stopped beside him.

"Hi, Gracie. What brings you?"

"Jack. You have to come to my house," Gracie said. "Something's going on. That nice Detective Willow came and asked me to pick you up and take you home until she and that asshole get there."

"Gracie, Gracie, Gracie," Jack said shaking his head. "I seriously doubt she called him an asshole. They wouldn't tell you why, huh?"

"No, but I think you might be in danger. She said she'd explain when they arrived." Gracie opened her trunk and began putting Jack's items in.

"I haven't said that I would, Gracie. Why are you loading my stuff?" His smile departed when he saw tears in her eyes. She was obviously distraught.

"You have to come, Jack," she said with a sniffle. "I don't want anything to happen to you. If there's no danger, I'll bring you back right away. I promise."

Jack hesitated only a few seconds. He certainly couldn't have Gracie crying. He stood and picked up his duffel, which was too heavy for the petite little lady, and laid it atop the other items in the trunk. He pushed his cart behind the dumpsters. "I suppose I could use a shower. Thanks, Gracie."

Gracie started the car and began driving around the buildings to the front. There was no conversation during the circle, so Jack knew what was coming. When she reached the main road, it started.

"Jack, I have an idea. I know you won't come and live with me, although I don't share your reasoning. I have a very nice back yard. We could pitch a tent or build a lean-to, and you would only have to come inside for showers or to pick up your meal. You could even eat outside, if you want."

"Gracie," Jack began. Then, after gathering his thoughts, "I love you like a granddaughter, but seeing me several hours a day, compared to once in a while, will change our relationship. That's not the only reason. I don't want an address."

He paused, unsure if what he was about to say would hurt a beautiful and kind young woman. He wrestled with the words for a time, and decided the best way to put her mind at ease was to just say it.

"If I get a job and have an address, I will also have to pay taxes to the Government that drafted me and my friends into that God-forsaken war and then failed to support us. On top of that, there would be no way to avoid the television and that worthless media scum that convinced the American people what horrible human beings we were for serving our country.

"No, Gracie. I'm happy where I am. People treat me well. I serve a purpose in Historical with whoever needs my services, and believe it or not, even if it's just a sandwich or a cup of coffee, I'm paid well.

"I'm not a member of Panhandler's Inc., standing on a street corner with a sign. I can't deceive people that way. Even if they do deserve it for falling for the scam in the first place. Did you know, I worked my way downtown about a year ago and watched those people. It was the same people. All they did was change locations day to day, so their victims wouldn't recognize them. I talked to one of them about joining. You know what he told me? He makes forty thousand dollars a year. In a bad year. Do you make forty thousand dollars a year, Gracie?"

"I did one year, but I had two jobs that year. That makes me angry."

"Why?"

"Because it's deceitful."

"It's a job. It's just like telemarketing. They're not the problem. The people buying their story are the problem. One out of a thousand people listen to the spiel. One out of five thousand buy in. If no one gave the panhandlers any money or no one listened to the spiel, would they still exist?"

"I don't know."

"They're corporations. So, yes. I never saw those panhandlers at the end of their shift throw their signs in the trunk of a Mercedes, but I wouldn't be surprised. Praying on sympathy. No, Gracie. I'm happy where I am. No one will ever confuse me with them."

"I know, Jack. I know your wishes and I would like to respect them," Gracie said. Then, after a few moments' hesitation, she continued, "I guess I'm just selfish. I need you. I don't have anyone except Willie. He doesn't hold a conversation very well."

Jack laughed. "I would like to say I would meet you half way and stay with you a couple nights a week, but I won't. You know where to find me, Gracie. Any time you need conversation, just stop by."

"Sometimes you can be so hard-headed."

"I know, but you love me anyway."

"Yes, I do," Gracie said as she pulled into her driveway. "Did you finish your sandwich?"

"Yup. I'm good, unless you want to make me some coffee."

Gracie smiled. "Jack, have you ever heard of a Keurig?"

"That's one of them fancy coffee pots, right?"

"Yes. I have one. I'll show you how to use it and then you can make your own coffee."

Gracie and Jack walked into the house and Gracie locked the door behind her, steering Jack toward the back, opening the sliding glass door, where she pointed out her ample back yard. Jack smiled at her and gave her arm a squeeze. She then took him to the kitchen and showed him how to work the Keurig.

Jack heard Gracie's cell phone warble and watched as she walked away, answering. It must have been one of the detectives. Probably the female, because Gracie was being very polite and talking about having him at her house. When she finished the conversation, she returned to the kitchen.

"They're on their way, Jack. Probably about twenty minutes, she figured. Do you want to hop in the shower, or wait until they leave?"

"What are you saying? I stink?"

"Yes, you do. Because you won't move in here and keep me company. Not necessarily odor-wise."

Jack laughed again. "I'll need a change of clothes from your trunk."

Gracie handed him her car keys. "You know where everything's at. Have fun."

Jack took the keys and went to the garage, opened the trunk and began rummaging, looking for a complete set of clothes. He felt sorry for Gracie. She really wanted him to move in, but what would he do here, except breed contempt? He liked Gracie and he wanted to keep the relationship.

Ophidian

As it turned out, he wasn't going to have to wait for his wife to get home. Buying a new car was a lot easier than he'd thought. He had found the car on the internet, met the man, took the car for a test drive to the bank, got a cashier's check and dropped the man back off.

He didn't even bother going home. He went right to Historical and into a coffee shop across the street and a few buildings down from Arnold's. When he walked in the door, the first thing he did was check the tables by the window. Were they near enough to the window for the owner or manager to see Arnold's store? The coffee shop wouldn't have been opened yet, but the manager or owner may have been in early.

Ophidian stepped up to the counter to place an order. The young lady, with Alicia on her nametag, smiled a pretty smile and asked what he would like.

"I'll have a cup of medium roast, please," he answered.

"Okay. Coming right up," Alicia said. "Would you like anything to eat, today?"

"No, thank you. Say, what's with all the police the last couple of days?"

"Oh. There's no need to worry, sir. They've just stepped up the patrol recently. There was a robbery, yesterday morning. It was way before the rest of us were even awake, though."

"So, the dirtbag is going to get away totally free, huh? I hate it when people take things that don't belong to them."

"Well, I don't know about that. Our police department is pretty good. Plus, we have our own overnight security," Alicia said laughingly. "Soldier Jack keeps an eye on things around here."

Alicia turned around to pour his coffee, which was just as well. If he asked one person too many questions, it would arouse suspicion. He was going to accept his cup, gracefully, and continue to learn about this Soldier Jack from someone else in the area. He must be some sort of security hired by the businesses here to watch things overnight.

Ophidian took his coffee, issued a thank you and proceeded to the window counter where he took a seat. He scanned the businesses through the window to determine the best 'browsing' spot where he would, most likely, be asked if he needed help to find anything. That would open the door for conversations.

There were several antique businesses but he was never much on other people's junk. Also, an ice cream shop. He could go there but he would have to wait until he finished his coffee. A clothing store looked to be selling western wear. That would be the place.

He continued to scan the exterior area while he sipped his coffee. The police car was nowhere to be seen, right now. There was minimal foot traffic. There was, however, a woman in a police uniform walking the street, marking tires. He kept his eye on her. When she finished this block, he would cross the street and check out the clothing store.

Giving Birch something else to think about was another item on Ophidian's list. Hopefully, the detective still had the same phone number, otherwise he would have to break into his house again. The last time he did, Birch had been on a bender. Ophidian had made sure he had left nothing out of place. All he had wanted was a look at the file Birch was working on, which Ophidian hadn't found, but he had found a telephone number registry and he had gotten his phone number from that. He had also snapped a few photos of framed family pictures Birch had around.

The meter gal had cleared the block, so Ophidian finished his coffee, discarded the cup and went outside. Since this was Historical, just about everyone jaywalked, but he wasn't taking any chances. He walked to the corner and crossed on the crosswalk. He stood outside the shop, looking at the boots and hats in the window display before entering, because that's just what people did.

Having spent sufficient time window-shopping, he entered the store, went to the cowboy hat section and began picking up and replacing different styles. He was beginning to wonder if anyone was going to come to his aid. He had been in this section for several minutes.

"Good morning. Looking for a new dome cover?"

About time. "I am," Ophidian said with a smile. "The sun this summer just about did me in."

"Yeah. It was pretty bad this year," replied the clerk. "Do you have a particular style in mind?"

"Shady." Ophidian continued with the smile.

"Okay. I take that to mean no particular style. How about this Cattleman? It's on sale this week. Ninety-nine dollars and it's yours."

"That sounds like a good price," Ophidian said, turning the hat around, as if examining it. "By the way, have you seen Soldier Jack lately?"

"Nah., He doesn't come around much anymore, now that Arnold's is closed. Probably getting his meals on the south end."

Homeless!

"Well, I promised him a coffee. I'll pop over there. You're a good salesman. I'll take this hat."

Ophidian bought the hat, exited the store and walked to his car. He threw the hat into the back seat, started the engine and began slowly cruising Historical, heading south. He checked all roads and alleys as he passed them and was about to turn around and try again, when that cop approached from his front. The cop's head was on a swivel, as he eyed every business and cross street himself.

As he passed by Ophidian's car, Ophidian waved. The cop waved back. Ophidian continued on, watching his rearview mirror. He saw the cop slowing, looking back at him. *Shit!*

The cop looked like he might be looking for a way to turn around. Maybe. Maybe not. Ophidian wasn't going to take any chances. He hung a right and began his usual zigzag escape from the area. He had shaved. What the hell had alerted the cop? Damnit! Cops were trained to be observant. Was Ophidian going to have to get another car?

Shit. The damn cop was closing behind him. *Don't give him a reason to stop you. Stay calm. Continue at the speed limit and don't make any overt moves.* Ophidian continued along Third until he came to a stoplight. The cop pulled to a stop behind him. When the light turned green, Ophidian drove through the intersection and the cop's lights flicked on. Ophidian pulled over right away. He didn't have any of his guns with him. This might get sticky. He rolled down his window and waited.

"Good afternoon, sir," the officer said. "I pulled you over for displaying expired tags. Could I see your license, registration and proof of insurance, please?"

Ophidian smiled. "I can provide one of those. I've just bought the car, and stopped to get a coffee and a hat, and was on my way to the house to get what I needed for the DMV." Ophidian pointed at the hat in the back seat.

"No problem. I'll take the license. I can get the other information off the plates. I'll have to issue a fix-a-ticket, though. Once you get your new temps, you can toss it. In the meantime, keep it in your car, in case you're stopped again."

"I will do that," Ophidian said. Was this a stroke of luck? Had he simply been stopped for a traffic violation? He was going to have to get the car registered as quickly as possible to avoid another stop.

Birch

When Travis walked out of the courthouse, he found Willow in the same place he had left her. In the car. Conducting phone interviews and digging on the tablet. The woman was relentless, which in her line of work was a good thing.

"Tell me you have something," Travis said as he dropped into the driver's seat.

"According to the coroner, Arnold Bayer was in good health, prior to his death. So, no mercy killing. There have been no recent changes to his life insurance policy, and surprisingly, the policy is not for a large amount of money, but who knows what a large amount of money is to an insurance company? Not one of the employees was any help at all. I talked to Gracie. There were no deliveries scheduled that day, and "Pervy" is not allowed in the store prior to opening. A nickname given to your CI by Gracie, Isabel and Lisa."

Willow looked at him with a grin. "I'm not certain your man is going to make a credible witness, if it comes to it."

"I also called all my CIs, explained the situation and asked them to call me if they hear anything. When I saw you coming down the steps, I called Gracie and told her we would be about twenty minutes, and lastly, I called Mrs. Bayer. Her sister answered the phone and said Mrs. Bayer is staying at her house and finally fell asleep, and she wants to keep her that way."

Travis started the car and pulled out into traffic in the direction of Blankenship's house, rubbing his forehead in frustration. He then pounded the steering wheel. "Damnit! I was sure it was for the insurance."

"Travis, we may not know the why until we get Mrs. Bayer to fess up. In all likelihood, the killer doesn't know. If he is a hired gun, he wouldn't care."

Willow was right. It was time to stop focusing on the why until things became more concrete. He didn't even have any proof that the wife had hired a killer. His focus should be on finding the killer. He was going to have to start thinking like a woman who wanted her husband killed but was too weak to poison him.

"You're a woman," he announced to his partner, but he hesitated too long before explaining.

"Shit, Travis. How did you manage to come upon that epiphany?"

Travis snarled in her direction but kept his eyes focused on the road. "If you'd give me a minute to explain, I was going to ask you to put yourself in the wife's position. For whatever reason, you want your husband dead, but you don't want to do it yourself. What would you do? You'd find someone to do it for you. Not someone you know, though, because you don't want your friends and family to know you're capable of such atrocities. What would be your first step?"

"Hmm. TOR?"

"Exactly. Call research. See if they have a way to find out who her internet provider is. Maybe the provider can tell us if they know what search engines she uses. Come to think of it, maybe it's in the husband's name."

Willow started to dial but Travis stopped her. "Hold off until we leave Blankenship's. If you're on the phone, that will leave me to deal with crabby."

"I don't find her the least bit crabby."

Travis knew another dig into his demeanor was coming. He gave Willow a stern look but didn't invite the dig. She just returned his stern look. She continued the stare-down as he pulled to the curb in front of Blankenship's. Then she widened her eyes, followed by a wink as she exited the cruiser. He suddenly felt like Rodney Dangerfield.

He followed Willow to the front door, where Blankenship was waiting. Gracie gave Willow a warm, inviting smile. Not so much for Travis, but she did hold the door open as he passed through.

"Jack is in the shower," Gracie offered. "Would you like coffee, or soda? I have bottled water, too."

"I wouldn't mind a water," Willow responded, then, saving Gracie from asking him, "Travis?"

"A water sounds good. Thank you, Gracie," Travis answered.

Gracie stopped short, looking back at Travis. "You and I are never going to be friends, Detective. You can call me Ms. Blankenship."

"That's enough, Gracie," Willow said sternly. "It's our job to ask questions. Sometimes those questions are going to offend. Travis and I are trying to find the person who killed Arnold. We will do what it takes to that end."

Gracie stared at Willow. Willow stared back. Gracie sighed with remorse. "I know. I'm sorry, Detective. Jack didn't kill Arnold. I know you know that now. It's just that he's so important to me. People don't respect veterans of that war, especially the homeless ones." Gracie continued to the refrigerator, pulled out two bottles of water and handed Travis his bottle first.

While waiting for Jack, Gracie and Willow engaged in small talk and Gracie even tried to include Travis but he was only half-listening, still trying to figure out a way to get the wife to admit what she had done and tell them who the killer was. He smiled and answered as best he could when his name was mentioned.

After nearly five minutes, Jack emerged. Not wanting to exclude Jack's semi-adopted granddaughter, Travis asked Jack to sit at the table, so he could brief him on why he asked Gracie to pick Jack up.

As Jack joined them, Travis admired him. The man's expression never changed. He never looked worried, or angry, or sad. He looked content, which surprised Travis, considering his homeless status. Travis decided to lead with something off his original topic.

"Jack, have you applied for entitlements at the VA?"

"I did many years ago, but I was denied rather quickly. Why?"

"Things have changed, Jack. You should re-apply."

"Have they? Their focus is on immigration. They didn't care about us then and they don't care about us now."

"Okay. Well, it's your decision but I will go on record as disagreeing. Jack, the reason we asked Ms. Blankenship,
. . ."

"Gracie," Gracie interrupted.

Travis smiled at her. ". . . Gracie to pick you up is because we think there might be an element of danger involved in your being outside so much. We have a strong feeling that this was a murder for hire and the killer may have seen us in our investigation. He bolted when we gave chase and eluded us, but now he knows we have information and he will try to find out what that information is."

"What could he find out?" Gracie asked.

"He could ask questions down at Historical," Willow answered. "And someone there might mention Jack, thinking the killer is just an opportunity to gossip."

Gracie nodded and her expression led Travis to believe she was trying to decide who would do that. His attention went back to Jack.

"We're arranging to put you up in a safe house, at no charge, until we can get this guy put away. What I'm going to ask is that you don't leave and put yourself out there. If you need groceries, Willow or I will grab them for you. I couldn't get officers to stay with you, because frankly, we don't have that many."

"He can stay with me," Gracie nearly shouted out. "Jack, you can stay here."

"Gracie," Travis said before Jack could respond, "people at Historical know of your relationship with Jack. I would suggest that you distance yourself until we catch the guy, and I would also suggest that you stay with a friend or relative for a bit."

"I'm not afraid of that prick. I can take care of myself."

"Then get afraid, Gracie," Willow added. "This is not a game. He's a killer. Cold-blooded. And being a woman won't help you."

"Wouldn't it be wiser for me to be out there?" Jack asked. "Wouldn't that draw him out and make it easier to catch him?"

"Yeah," Travis answered, "if this were a movie. We don't do bait, Jack. We don't put people in harm's way."

"What if I don't want to live in a safe house?"

Willow answered bluntly, "The guy finds you, kills you. Our only witness is dead. He walks free and continues to kill."

"It's okay if you want to sugar-coat that a little bit," Jack said, smiling.

"There's no sugar to be found, Jack," Travis added. "We need you to do this for us. We'll work as fast as we can."

"Okay," Jack said. "I can't have Gracie in danger. I will, but I want a phone. That way I can keep you two on your toes."

"Thank you, Jack." Travis laughed. "We don't have nearly enough people telling us our job. I'll get you a phone. Can you stay with Gracie tonight? The house should be ready tomorrow."

Jack looked at Gracie. "I suppose I can. If I really have to."

Gracie laughed and acted hurt. "Thanks, Jack. Just for that, when you move into the safe house, you get to take Willie. I'll go to my sister's. She doesn't like dogs."

Travis and Willow thanked the two and excused themselves. Travis knew it was getting late in the day. The wife was obviously not going to be available, and he would need to give Vicki time to get the safe house and warrants ready.

He was a little concerned about tonight. He didn't know how desperate the killer was. If he was intent on killing witnesses and spent the time trying to find Jack, there would be nothing to stop him except that seventy-year-old veteran and a five-foot-four, one-hundred-and-ten-pound woman. Travis shook it off. No one could be that fast. "There's not much more we can do without that warrant. We'll call it a night and start out tomorrow morning with the wife, the safe house, Carver's brother and research. Maybe they have something that would help us get a search warrant."

"Sounds good," Willow responded. "I'll meet you at the station at six in the morning."

"You might meet someone there but it won't be me that early."

Ophidian

He had spent the best part of the afternoon at the DMV getting his temporary plates. Having finally got through the ridiculous lines, his car was now legal. It didn't matter. The new car was in the driveway, which was where it would sit until tomorrow. He had made arrangements for a paint job on his old car, as well as a complete detailing. Then he would sell it.

Now he was in his wife's car. He had told her he needed to buy a new car because his had broken down on him. As a result, he had fallen behind at work and would use her car to get caught up.

He made a stop at a Save Mart and picked up a box of crackers, a package of cookies, a novel and two magazines. Then he began the drive back to Historical. He wasn't going to have trouble with the officer who had seen him earlier. It was shift-change time. He would make a quick pass through the rear areas, and if he didn't find the guy, he would park and start asking.

It was a little late in the day for coffee, so he started behind the ice cream shop. Slowly, he made his way through the back, but saw no signs of a homeless man. He crossed the street and had no better luck, but there was a man hauling bags of garbage to the dumpster. Ophidian drove up to him.

"Hey. How ya doin?" he asked the man.

"Good. How are you?"

"Doing well. Thanks. Say, I'm looking for Jack. Have you seen him around?"

"He was here earlier but Gracie picked him up. I think she took him to dinner. She's weird that way."

"Gracie?" Ophidian asked, displaying a confused look.

"Blankenship. She used to work at Arnold's."

"Oh, yeah? Too bad about that guy. You have any idea where she normally takes him?"

"Nah. Max might know. He used to work there too. He works across the street now. At the UPS store. They close in about ten minutes, though, so you'd better hurry."

"I will do that. Thanks for your help. Have a nice night."

"You too."

Ophidian was pretty sure there was no dinner involved. The guy had seen Ophidian in some way. He was certain that Gracie person had been asked to house him until they caught Ophidian but they were not going to catch Ophidian. He was going to give Birch something else to think about but he would have to purchase a burner first.

He pulled away, quickly, but not ridiculously so. Leaving the alley and turning left on Third, he continued across Historical instead of turning in front of the UPS store. He drove for about six blocks, which brought him to a retail shopping center. He turned into the Walmart parking lot, pulled into a stall and shut his engine off.

Pulling out his phone, he loaded his white pages app and did a search on Gracie Blankenship. There were four Blankenships but only one had a G in front of it. He wrote down the address, stuck it in his pocket and walked into Walmart to get a burner.

After making his purchases, he loaded the Blankenship address into his TomTom GPS. He wouldn't use his phone, because that would draw suspicion if he was ever caught. The TomTom loaded and he proceeded with the directions given.

He was directed to an older section of the city, as evidenced by the poor condition of the fencing. He guessed seventies or eighties. The street he was looking for was three blocks deep from the main road. He turned on the street and proceeded at a reasonable speed, keeping his head facing forward but his eyes watching addresses. The house he was looking for was halfway down the block on the right. There was nothing special about it. The tree in the front, along with the shrubbery, were pretty much the same as the rest.

He switched his focus to the houses on each side. They were both occupied. Continuing his speed along the street, he counted houses to the next cross street, took the first right and drove to the next street over and took another right. Luck was with him. There was a 'for sale' sign on a house about the same distance down as the

Blankenship home. It was going to be one house off but he could live with that.

Satisfied, he left the area and headed home. Tonight, he would make one pass through Historical and look for the homeless guy. He didn't think he was going to find him there. Birch was too cautious. He would be staying with the Blankenship woman. If not, she would know where she dropped him off. He would have to do her, too, but what's one more notch?

After he took care of the homeless guy and the wife, there would be no more witnesses. He would take that opportunity to send Birch a few photos with an appropriate warning attached. Having finished that, he would be home free. He was definitely going to have to restrict his hobby to out-of-town jobs from here on, though. It was getting too hot here.

Sturgeon

Willow left Travis to finish a little file clean-up and drove home to meet with Mark. Mark hadn't arrived yet. Kris hadn't, nor had any of her exercise buddies. She would forgo her workout for the day and hop in the shower.

When she finished, she wrapped a towel around her and hurried to the door to make sure no one was waiting on the stoop. No one was. She unlocked the door and went to her room to dress. While she was deciding what to wear, she heard the front door open and close. One of three things was about to happen. She would hear bustling around in the kitchen, which would mean Kris, or she would hear the treadmill going, which would mean one of her friends, or. . .

Mark came through her bedroom door. "Hi, honey."

"Hey, you. How much can you tell me?"

"Oh, this isn't all that top secret. What do you want to know?" Mark asked as he followed his naked girlfriend around her room.

Willow began to dress. "I want to know everything. I'm a woman, remember?"

Mark laughed. "Well, I can tell you that I was implicated as the mole by Horace but I don't think they really believed that. They grilled me, though. I think that was just in case I was in cahoots with Lisa."

"Cahoots?" Willow laughed. "Well, ya'll is funny."

"They got her, just before she crossed the Canadian border. She admitted I wasn't involved. She won't tell them where Chulo is, though. They practically offered her a walk and she still wouldn't say."

"I can't say as I blame her. Look at Sander's outcome." Willow heard pots rattling and knew Kris had arrived. She quickly buttoned her blouse, knowing who was going to be charging through her bedroom door.

"Auntie!" both kids screamed in unison as they clasped her in hugs.

"Hi, guys." Willow hugged them back. "I have to talk to Uncle Mark. Why don't you two check to see if Pepper needs to go outside?" The kids darted out of the room, calling Pepper's name.

"So," Willow continued, "who's the new boss? Have you met him or her yet?"

"No clue. They had other things to think about. We're all grounded for a couple weeks, anyway. We'll have to go through exit interviews and Psych meetings. They're going to have to know how each of us feels about Lisa leaving."

"Yeah. That makes since, I guess."

"What are you guys working on? Solve that Howard case yet?"

"Arnold. I knew you weren't listening to me."

"I was listening," Mark retorted defensively. "The stabbing, right?"

"Oh, for crying out loud. Go get the car. We're taking yours. I'm going to go greet everyone. I'll be out in a minute."

"Just one more thing," Mark said. When Willow turned back to him, he was on his knee, ring extended. "Will you marry me? "

Willow's hands flew over her face and she screamed. Even knowing it was coming, he had taken her by surprise. Loud, thunderous tromping could be heard outside the room and three of her friends charged through the door, ready for a fight. One of those friends, Kris, mimicked Willow's reaction. The other two just groaned and went back to the exercise room.

"Yes," Willow cried. "You know I will. I love you."

Mark put the ring on Willow's finger and the two embraced, Willow admiring the ring. Kris stroked her hair and congratulated her and then left to return to her kitchen preparations.

"We need to go," Mark said. "It's almost six and it's a twenty-minute drive." Willow walked beside him, but she continued to admire the ring. Even though she had already seen it, it hadn't been on her finger. Being the gentleman, he opened the car door for her and she took a seat, being careful not to catch the ring on the upholstery. She knew she was being ridiculous but she had never been engaged before and it was going to take some getting used to.

She caught him several times looking over at her admiring the ring while he was driving. She laughed and told him to stop watching her, and he, likewise, told her it was just a ring and stop staring at it.

The drive did take twenty minutes but they found a parking place rather easily. They made their way into the terminal, found the staircase to baggage and descended the stairs. There was a flight board at the bottom of the stairs, and she saw Amy's flight was on time. They took a seat by the baggage carousel assigned to her flight.

Mark held Willow's hand while they waited. Her problem was he was holding the wrong hand. He had the hand with the ring, and she didn't know how she was going to get him to switch hands without sounding like a dork. How was anyone supposed to admire her ring if his hand was covering it?

She quickly jumped up and moved to his other side, picking a magazine up off the end table. She sat down with the magazine on his other side and grabbed his hand with her ringless hand but he shook it off and reached for her left hand again, covering the ring. She looked at him. He was brandishing a smirk. She elbowed him in the arm and he let out a laugh.

"You're not funny," she admonished.

"I kind of am," he retorted but he just held her right hand, showing he was finished teasing her.

Willow replaced the magazine, not really interested in muscle cars, and leaned her head onto his arm. "I said I love you, today, right?"

"Not that I remember, but you've mentioned that I don't listen to you, so. . ."

"You really don't. Otherwise you would know I've said it several times already."

"This was the second time. I don't think that constitutes 'several'."

The bags began descending onto the carousel and passengers were flowing into baggage claim, so Willow sat up and looked for Amy. Amy saw her before she saw Amy, and began walking toward the duo. Willow stood and scratched her chin with her left hand, and Amy let out a yelp and smiled wide, running at them.

"Congratulations, Will," Amy said, clasping on the routine Gaudier hug, albeit a little bone-crunching. "I'm so happy for you."

"Thank you," Willow said, allowing Amy to touch her ring.

"This is cause for a celebration. No one's home, right now, so I'm taking you two to dinner. No arguments."

Willow knew better than to argue with a Gaudier but it would have done no good, anyway. Amy's smile had disappeared and she was staring at Mark. "Don't mess this up, Maxwell. I can hurt you."

Mark smiled. "I know you can. I remember the bashing you handed that detective."

Amy blushed with remorse for the disfigurement she had caused Willow that day, but she collected herself and flat-handed Mark on the chest. "It's best you don't forget."

Amy pointed out her two bags to Mark. He collected them off the carousel and they were off to the parking area, Mark carrying the bags. The girls walked ahead, chatting about wedding plans, school, Minnesota weather and a variety of other topics. Apparently, he was going to the Gaudiers' for Thanksgiving dinner, whether he liked it or not.

Willow sat in the back with Amy as they continued their discussion. Amy discussed how many credits she needed to obtain her degree. How she was coping with the snow. How often she spoke to assorted family members. Willow was surprised when she learned that neither Amy nor Missy had spoken to their father while they were away at school. She wasn't sure why she was surprised, considering how busy the man was and the fact that he seldom saw the inside of the mansion, but still. He couldn't find time for his kids? Willow decided she didn't ever want to be filthy rich.

Willow also knew, despite their age difference, that she was probably closer to Amy than anybody, so she asked, "How would you feel about being my maid of honor?"

"Really? I would love to. Are you sure? I mean, heck yeah, I will. I know a male stripper, and everything."

Mark laughed, but when he saw Amy's stoic expression in the rear-view mirror, he commented, "The hell, you say."

"He's so easy," Amy said to Willow with a wink.

"Oops. I almost forgot," Willow said, pulling her phone from her pocket. She snapped a picture of the ring and sent it off in a text.

Birch

Travis continued his internet search for puppies, as well as sifting through the cold case files, but he set both aside when he received the text from Willow. It was a photo. He was looking at the biggest rock he had ever seen. Holy cow. How much do these FBI agents make, anyway?

He realized what time it was, and how he had not only missed his workout, but also dinner. He texted Kris.

{You still there?}

{Yup. Doin dishes.}

{Don't lock up. Be there in a bit.}

{Kids are playing with Pepper. You can help me separate them.}

{Ten minutes.}

He quickly grabbed his gear and darted for the garage. As he was driving, his thoughts went to Jack and the odds of him using the cell phone Travis would get him to call people other than himself, Willow or Gracie. As long as he didn't say where he was, it shouldn't be a problem. Travis made a mental note to make sure to discuss safety and security with the man.

Gracie might end up being a small problem. She didn't seem to like not knowing where Jack was. Willow had a good rapport with Gracie, though, and could explain the need for secrecy.

Travis knew, if he could get into the Bayer home, he could find something to use as leverage to get Mrs. Bayer to admit her involvement. It was going to be sticky, but he had been in sticky spots many times before.

He arrived at Willow's and walked in to find Salt draped over the back of the couch, uncaring about anything. Pepper, on the other hand, was very much enjoying the attention he was getting from the kids.

"Did you guys get your reading done, today?" he asked them.

"No," Macy answered with gumby shoulders.

"Not yet," Ashton echoed.

"Okay. Get to it and leave the poor dog alone. He looks worn out."

Travis knew his kids would do as they were told, so he gave Kris a peck on the cheek and went to the exercise room. While he was on the leg press, his mind went back to the case. There was still no proof that it was a murder-for hire. He knew it was, though. The lack of evidence told him the killer was practiced at it. He didn't seem to make mistakes. The only way to actually catch the killer was to find the person who had hired him. It would be a her. Travis was positive about that. Women, however, usually used other means to kill. Poison, mostly, but he was sticking with his feelings that Mrs. Bayer didn't have the stomach for it.

He was going to have to hope the killer made a mistake by asking too many questions. He had already talked to Maynard. Warned him on what to listen for. Curiosity questions were one thing but specific questions about witnesses, etc., were something else.

He needed to find a way to get his mind off the case for a couple of hours. His thoughts were becoming stagnant. If he could clear his mind, he might be able to come up with some fresh ideas. He had talked with Kris about a puppy. She had thought it was a great idea. The kids wouldn't be so insistent on her having a need to go to Willow's all the time.

Both kids were really good with Pepper. Travis' concern about them hurting a poor little puppy seemed to be unfounded. He was going to draw the line at a cat, though. As cute as they were as kittens, they turned into a totally different animal when they grew up. Travis didn't need to be used as a scratching post.

His workout was done, so he went to see if there were any leftovers. To his surprise, Kris already had a plate of food sitting at the table. He thanked her and dug in hungrily.

"Any luck with Pet Farm?" she asked.

"Depends," he answered between bites. "Pet Farm is an adoption agency. Puppies are not their forte. How strong do we feel that it has to be a puppy?"

"I think a smaller dog would be fine, as long as it's not too old. I'd hate to have to go through that loss with them so soon."

"They don't have a Papillon, but they have a beagle and a couple of other breeds that are smaller. I've always liked beagles."

"Let's take them down, this weekend, and have them decide."

"That's a great idea. They'll take ownership that way," Travis agreed. "By the way," he continued, "did you see the size of that rock on Will's finger?"

"Yes. In person, actually. It's beautiful."

"Kind of makes me wonder how much FBI agents make," Travis snickered.

"Oh, for Pete's sake, Travis. It could have been bought on a time plan. It could have been he has been saving money for several years. It might have nothing to do with his salary."

"Hmm. You're right. Maybe he stole it."

Kris smacked the back of his head as she picked up his plate to wash it. He quickly snatched the roll and continued to eat. "When I finish washing this plate, the kids and I are going home. Make sure you lock up," Kris announced.

"I'm leaving, too. I'll shower at home."

"Okay. Let Pepper out one more time before you leave."

Travis stood and let Pepper charge through the door, and he took a seat on one of the patio chairs and waited for the dog to finish his business. When Pepper came running back to the patio, Travis let him in and found that Kris and the kids had already left. He locked the patio door and locked the front door as he left, too.

As he drove home, he caught himself several times with his mind wandering to the case. He deliberately would admire the construction of a particular building or criticize someone's driving abilities. He was determined to keep his mind clear and would continue to do so until tomorrow morning.

Kris had agreed that adoption of a dog was probably a better way to go. When he got home, he was going to get active in his search.

As he arrived home, he was surprised to have beaten Kris. The garage was empty. He pulled in and went, right away, to his computer and began looking up pet adoption locations near his house. He found several and began writing down phone numbers on his desk pad. The door to the garage opened and he heard Macy's lighter feet charging toward his den.

"Daddy, can we get a dog?"

"No, honey. They make too much of a mess in the back yard," Travis answered, digging for a commitment.

"We can clean up the messes, Dad," Ashton offered, arriving quickly.

"What happens when you get tired of cleaning up those messes?"

"We won't," both kids offered in unison.

"Okay. I'll tell you what. I'll talk to Mom . . ."

"We already asked her. She said to talk to you," Macy ratted out.

What the . . . "Okay, then. I'll make a few calls and see what kind of dogs keep noisy little rug rats in line."

"Daddy!" Macy scowled with her hands on her hips.

"Oh. I'm sorry. Did I say that out loud?"

Macy wrapped her arms around her dad's leg and began tugging him off his chair. Ashton joined in, pulling his dad's arm. Travis, slowly, eased off the chair and to the floor, being careful not to hurt his children, and the wrestling match began.

Kris entered from the kitchen, folding her arms across her chest and shaking her head. "I hope you didn't need anything from the store. I had to stop and get milk."

"No, I'm good," Travis grunted out. "You can fetch my bath, though."

Kris's eyes widened and her jaw dropped. "Did you just tell me to fetch?" she let out a roar and charged into the fray, locking Travis' head. "I've got him, guys. Pull his ears off."

"Whoa," Travis said. "Wait. What? Ow, let go of my ears, you little gremlins."

Sturgeon

McCallister's was packed. Willow was surprised, this close to Thanksgiving, but then she realized that there was about to be a large spread on many tables across America, and whoever was doing the cooking probably wanted nothing to do with it until then. Leave it to a Gaudier to pick one of the most expensive restaurants in Carpel.

It also wasn't much of a surprise that every single member of the staff referred to Amy as Miss Gaudier. Willow could only guess how much Amy and the rest of her family would dine at this well-known and respected establishment. Even the manager called her Miss Gaudier. Usually the manager would try to impress guests by remembering their first names.

"Have you decided on a wedding planner yet?" Amy asked as they were seated in an elevated booth that Willow didn't even know existed.

"Of course not, Amy. Mark's just asked me before we got in the car to pick you up. I think we have time. Unless there's something he hasn't told me." Willow looked at Mark and back at Amy. "We haven't even picked a date yet."

"Okay. Well, it can't be the sixth of June. Tony's getting married on the sixth and the whole family will be there, naturally."

"Really? I'm so happy for him." Willow felt a little hurt that she hadn't received an invitation. Maybe if she dropped a subtle hint. "I wasn't aware. I haven't seen him in months, though, so that's probably why."

Amy smirked. "Nice, Will. They're a little late getting invitations out. They had a problem with the photographer and Mom fired the guy."

Okay, maybe it wasn't so subtle.

"Which is why," Amy continued, "I asked if you had a wedding planner. That's how Mom met Daddy. She was the wedding planner for Aunt Brie's wedding. She might be a little hurt if you don't ask her."

The server arrived to take their drink order. Willow asked for a glass of Merlot and then the server looked toward Mark. "And for you, sir?" Mark looked surprised to be asked before Amy, but he responded with a Jack and Coke. Then the server looked toward Amy. "For you, Miss Gaudier?"

"I'll have a glass of Chardonnay, Melody. Thank you."

The server left to get the drinks and Willow just had to know, so she asked, "Okay, Amy. What's going on? You're away at school nine months out of the year. How is it that everyone and their mother here knows you?"

"Well, Will. . . You're a detective. Why do you think they know me? I'll give you a hint. I only eat here maybe once every two years."

"Your dad is the owner," Mark offered.

Amy dipped her finger in her water glass and flicked it at Mark. "That is so not on the mark, Mark, and if you will, Will is not your name." Amy looked back at Willow.

Willow had also thought that Amy's dad might be the owner. Then it dawned on her. Her jaw dropped so far, she thought it might hit the table. "You own McCallister's? You're only twenty-four years old."

"Yes, I am, and yes, I do. Daddy taught us well. I also own three McDonald's franchises, two salons, and an Ace Hardware franchise. Tony owns a golf club and a ski resort in Colorado. And Missy owns a Lexus dealership."

Willow was speechless. Mark looked to be somewhat intimidated. Willow found herself. "Here I was worried about you, when you left the house, only taking with you the four-hundred-thousand your dad had started off with."

"It's okay to be worried," Amy said. "I sure as heck am. We were all taught well. The businesses we own have to carry us forward. Dad will give us the 400K but then that will be it. If something goes wrong with our investments, right now, he will help us, but once we're out, we're out. We will have to succeed or fail on our own merit. It sounds so horrible when there are people living paycheck to paycheck, but there's a lot more to this than you might think."

"Like what?" Mark asked.

"Like even though one of my salons made a two-thousand-dollar profit in the first quarter this year, it actually lost money. That particular salon usually makes twenty-five hundred a quarter, so it's working at a loss."

"That doesn't make sense," Willow responded.

"Like I said," Amy offered, "there's more to this than you might think. I guess if I was worried about one of us, it would be Missy. Dad always told us to never put all our eggs in one basket, and she has one basket. I asked her about it before we went back to school. She just said she had this and I should mind my own businesses."

Amy was not being a braggart. Willow had been the one who'd brought it up. She had known Amy for many months, and the woman never spoke of her investments. She never projected herself as better than others. She was polite to everyone. She had anger issues, but she was working hard on that. Willow would be an idiot not to be envious, but if there was ever anyone who deserved to be filthy rich, it was the Gaudiers, to the one. They were almost too kind, if that were even possible.

"So, what are you guys thinking, date-wise?" Amy asked, changing the subject.

"Amy. He's literally just asked me when we were heading to pick you up. We have nothing for you right now. How about you? Any signs you might be a Mrs. pretty soon?"

Amy sighed. "Alas, no. There are a couple that are interested in me, but I can't reciprocate. One, you can't even see his skin because he's tatted head to foot, the other just doesn't seem to have any drive. I feel nothing when I'm out with either. I like a friend of Tony's, actually, but he doesn't even know I exist."

"Have you spoken to Tony about him? If he knows Tony, he might think you're above him."

"If he knows Tony, then he knows we don't think along those lines. Besides, he has a little money himself, so that's not an issue."

Willow nodded absently, then looked over at Mark. "You are kind of quiet. Nothing to add?"

Mark laughed. "I know better. I'm listening, but a man needs to know his place in these kinds of conversations."

"Good point," said Willow.

"Spot-on," said Amy.

The drinks were brought out and the server took their orders. Willow, now knowing Amy to be the owner, had been watching to see if she was studying her employees, but she wasn't. Her focus was on Willow and Mark. She wondered what Amy's employees thought of their boss.

"Okay, Ames. I have another question. Why isn't this place called Gaudier's?"

"It was called McCallister's when I bought it. I bought the name, as well. My name's not on any of my businesses. I personally consider it pompous to attach my name to any of them. So does Missy. Her dealership is just

Carpel Lexus. Tony's golf course is North Coast Links, and his name isn't on the ski resort, either. Although the lodges bear his name.

"I have enough issues with people thinking I'm special," Amy continued. "It makes it really difficult making friends. If my name is plastered everywhere, I'll have no chance at all."

Ophidian

Ophidian's phone alarm went off at two A.M. He glanced over at his wife to make sure it hadn't wakened her and slowly got out of bed, so as not to disturb her. He didn't need questions from her right now. Local jobs were definitely out of the question from this moment forward. He didn't need the hassle.

He picked out his darkest clothes, shoes and his phone and tip-toed from the room, descending the stairs to the living room, where he began dressing. He attached his phone to his belt, after setting it to vibrate, slipped on his shoes and entered the garage.

Opening his secret cabinet, he pulled out his stolen and untraceable Glock and suppressor and sat them in his trunk and, slowly, backed out of the driveway and onto the street. He slipped the CD into the player. It was the same CD he used at every job. It was tradition with him. He put the car into gear and proceeded, first, to the client's house. That would be first. From there he would drive to the Blankenship home. He wasn't going to waste his time looking for the man at Historical. Ophidian knew he wouldn't be there.

He stuck to main roads. If he was seen driving in a residential area this time of the morning, the police would stop him. He only had the temp paper attached to his window. Usually, they would run the plates and make sure the car belonged in the area, but with no plates, he would definitely be stopped.

The Walgreens on Manchester and the Parkway was a twenty-four-hour store. That was his excuse in the event he was stopped. He needed cough drops for the tickle in his throat. Walgreens was only good for the client's house. The Blankenship house was the opposite direction. For that trip, he would need to use Walmart, and say he needed milk.

He arrived at the point he would need to turn off. He checked for patrol cars and saw none, so he made the turn. He drove down to the same intersection where the rookie detective had spotted him earlier, and glanced down the street. No one home. There were no cars in the driveway. Not even his target's. His client had told him the garage was full, and he would know Arnold was already at work if he drove by and saw the car gone.

He thought it strange that the woman wasn't there. Where the hell was she? Putting on a hurt act, probably. Staying at a friend or relative's place. Shit. Loose end. He would need to do a little digging. Frustrated, he drove through the intersection and made his way back to the main road.

Continuing to keep his eyes peeled for patrol units, he proceeded past his turnoff for home and headed in the direction of Blankenship's. He had been fortunate, so far, in not seeing any squads. This time of night there were usually three or four that patrolled residential streets, but there were also a couple that parked on the main roads, to be centrally located for emergencies.

There was another concern for when he arrived at Blankenship's. Dogs. He didn't care about the tag and totes. They usually stayed in the house, being pampered like children. Better than children, actually. His concerns lay with the larger variety. The barking dog was his worst enemy. Luckily, not many people kept them anymore. Today's adult was just too lazy to be a pooper scooper.

Having arrived in the area, he drove down the street that had the empty house with his window down, looking for lights on and listening for any noises. It was quiet. Eerily so. Perfect. He took a right at the end of the block and parked in the Walmart side lot. There were three other cars in these stalls. He took a stall between the others. He would need to walk almost an entire block, being exposed.

He opened his trunk and pulled out a dark jacket, donning it over his dark clothes and continuing to survey the area, slipped his Glock and suppressor into a baggie and stuck it into his left pocket. That way he could dispose of both in the blink of an eye, if it came to it.

Closing his trunk, he made one more quick view of the area and began the walk to the vacant house. As he walked, he studied the assorted houses. The windows. The doors. The fences. All, while keeping his eyes opened for the patrol units, or any lights on in any of the houses.

As he turned the corner onto the street with the vacant house, he did notice a light on down the street. He wouldn't be going that far, so it shouldn't be a problem. He watched. He watched everything, stayed silent and left the sidewalk, so his already silent steps would be even more muffled.

When he reached the vacant house, he stepped back off the lawns and onto the sidewalk so as not to leave footprints. He waited. Watched. Listened, and then slowly moved toward the house. He slid behind some unkempt hedges. While watching the road and houses, he slipped on his gloves and shoe coverings.

Removing his jacket, he pulled the Glock and suppressor from the baggie, folded the baggie and returned it to the pocket. Moving out from behind the hedge, he used his jacket to wipe the dirt where he had been standing. Then, after wiping the jacket on the grass, he folded it neatly and placed it out of sight, behind the hedge. He stuck the suppressor in his pocket and the Glock in his belt.

The fence was in bad shape. It would break easily. He decided to use the posts, not even trusting the 2x4's. Reaching over, he got a firm hold on the post and hoisted himself over the fence. He waited and listened. Nothing. Moving quickly, he covered the distance to the correct corner of the back fence silently.

Even standing on his toes, it would be hard to see into the back yard of the Blankenship home. He pulled his phone and set it to record. Slowly, he moved it over the top of the fence in a circular motion. Satisfied, he brought the phone back down and began viewing the video. No doghouse. No lights. Quiet. He scaled the fence and crouched and waited. And listened.

When he didn't sense any threat, he stood and took two steps forward, turned and carefully wiped the indentation from his jump. Placing his ski mask on, he moved slowly to the back of the home. Two sliding glass doors. One smaller than the other. That would be the master bedroom. He moved to the larger. No keyed entry. An interior lock only, and he hadn't brought his magnet.

Moving to the side of the house, he found the side garage door. That would be his true entry. He would find something in the garage to use for the slider, as his disguised entry. Moving to the garage door, he pulled out his set of lock picks and, working his magic, he was in, in less than a minute.

One car. Assorted tools. Many of which he could use on the slider. First things first. He checked the entry door. Not locked. Putting his picks away, he slowly opened the door, listening for a creak. The hinges were silent. He entered the house. He was in a laundry room. He moved slowly to the adjoining hallway and stopped, listening. Nothing.

Across the hall was the master. The door was only slightly ajar. The lights were off. He moved his head out and looked to the left. Another bedroom but it was empty. It looked like it was used for storage. He looked to the right, down the long hallway. Another room. Door closed. No sign of lights. He moved that direction.

When he reached the door, he put his ear to it. He heard heavy breathing. Too heavy for a woman. This was his guy. Twisting the knob slowly, he opened the door and slithered through. He approached the bed, stood at the foot and began attaching his suppressor to the Glock.

He heard a creak and froze. He turned, but he turned too late. He heard a whoosh and then he heard the bones in his knee crack, and felt the searing pain. His leg collapsed and he went down to a woman screaming, "Meet Matilda!"

He brought the Glock to bear down on her chest before the recoil, but there was no recoil. She swung back left-handed. He heard the bones crack in his hand, felt the searing pain and watched the Glock slide across the room into the wall, then heard the woman scream, "Oh. He was hit by the bitch."

He lifted his good leg to kick her and crawl to the Glock, but the woman screamed again, "Batter up!" He heard the bones crack in his ankle and felt the searing pain, and saw the woman raise the bat over her head, looking at his crotch. "Foul balls," she screamed.

Before she could swing, the sleeping man flew over his head and into her, knocking her to the floor. The two were screaming at each other.

"I'm going to kill him," the woman screamed.

"No, Gracie. The detectives want him," the man replied.

Ophidian pushed himself with his one good arm toward the Glock. It seemed to take forever, but the two kept wrestling for the bat. He was there. Two more inches. A knee came down on his back. A heavy knee. The old man, Soldier Jack, was strong. He grabbed the hand reaching for the gun and jerked it away, wrapping it behind Ophidian's back. He pulled the face mask off and shoved Ophidian's head into the carpet.

"What happened to your goatee, buddy?" the man asked.

Blankenship Rewind

Gracie couldn't sleep. Even though it was Jack, she wasn't used to other people in her house. She wasn't used to her bedroom door being closed. She now lay in her bed, with Willie cuddled beside her. Giving initial thought to flipping on the light and reading, she quickly dismissed the idea and tried to close her eyes and will herself to sleep.

She was concerned about suffering depression. She was out of work. Arnold was dead, and she had been the one who had to walk in on it. She had been rude to the detective, and the man that she admired so much might be the target of a killer. Earlier in life, her late teens, she had suffered depression when her parents had died in a tour bus accident.

Her sister, as well as a very understanding doctor, and some therapy sessions, had helped her through that. Now, she was starting to feel that anxiety return. That probably had a lot to do with her current sleepless state, as well.

Willie's head flew up and his ears perked as he looked toward the door. Gracie had a sudden feeling of glee as she realized Jack probably couldn't sleep either. She wouldn't have to hide out in her bedroom anymore. She slipped her feet over the edge of the bed and sat up. She didn't own a robe and she didn't own pajamas. She slept in her beach shorts and a braless t-shirt. She reached down and picked up her pullover and pulled it over her head.

Quietly, she snuck to the door and peered through, looking at Jack's door. It was closed, and someone, not Jack, was twisting the knob.

Shit. It was him!

She went quickly to her bed and picked up her bat. Returning to the door, she peered through again and saw the man had entered Jack's room.

Gracie slipped through her door and quickly down the hall. The man had his back to her and was doing something with his hands. She pulled the bat back, eyed his right knee and swung with all her might. "Meet Matilda," she screamed as the bat struck the knee.

Real time

Gracie was angry with Jack. The asshole had broken into her house. She had every right to kill him. As time passed, though, her adrenalin eased and her temper ceased. Jack was right. The detectives would want to know who'd hired him. Jack knelt on his back, now, having instructed her to call the police. She went and grabbed her phone and quickly returned to the room with her bat in hand. She dialed 9-1-1.

"9-1-1. What's your emergency?"

"Someone broke into my house. He had a gun."

"Is he still there? Are you safe?"

"Yes, and yes. I hit him with my bat and my friend is holding him down. We have the gun."

The operator read off Gracie's address, which surprised her, considering she was calling from her cell phone, and said they were on their way.

The man was hurtling angry words at Jack, but Jack just kept asking the man where his goatee was. The man kept screaming at Jack to get off his back, but Gracie thought that was meant literally as opposed to Jack's continuing with the same question.

The police must have set a record with response time, as they were there within minutes of her hanging up.

She ran to the door and opened it, letting them in. There were two, and once again she was stripped of Matilda.

The officer instructed Jack to get off the man, saying he wasn't going anywhere. One of the officers began questioning Jack, while the other surveyed the man's wounds and called for a bus. Gracie stood silent this time, remembering how she had treated the detective. Then something dawned on her.

"Should I call the detectives?"

"What detectives?" the officer questioning Jack asked.

"The two detectives looking for him. Sturgeon and. . . uh. . ."

"Birch," Jack added.

"Detective Birch is looking for this guy? How do you know it's him?" the officer asked.

Gracie began at the beginning, with Arnold's murder, and with the occasional interjection from Jack, related the story to the officer.

"He's going to be in the hospital for a while," the officer replied. "We'll leave them a message. There's no need to wake them."

The officer stepped away for a minute and made a phone call. The other officer was pulling everything out of the pockets of the man on the floor. Another officer showed up and went to the officer emptying pockets, and the two began a muffled conversation that she couldn't hear. The gun had disappeared. She guessed the officer must have pocketed it.

The officer on the phone returned and asked her if she was the owner of the home. She replied that she was and he related that he was going with the ambulance and his patrol unit would be parked out front for a bit but someone would pick it up shortly. He also said the crime scene unit would be here in about a half hour.

The officer went back to his questions for Jack, and she guessed her turn would be coming soon. She felt like she wasn't being very useful with so much attention being paid to Jack and the asshole. She asked if anyone wanted coffee or water. They all said they were okay, but Jack wanted her away from the scene and asked her to make some coffee.

On her way to the kitchen to turn on the Keurig, the EMTs came through the front door and she pointed them in the right direction. She punched the button and filled the hopper with water, and took a seat at her island counter.

With the Keurlg heated, she stood and went to the cupboard, pulling out a cup for Jack and brewing him a cup. She heard the killer screaming obscenities as the EMTs wheeled him out of the room, handcuffed to the gurney. There wasn't much they could do here as the injuries were broken bones. The officer walked behind the gurney, and she watched as they all departed her home.

Jack came out and joined her at the island, accepting the coffee with a thank you. He stared at her. "I'm worried about you, Gracie."

"I'm fine, Jack. Really."

"Gracie, don't get me wrong. You saved my life and I appreciate it." He hesitated, looked at his coffee and then back at her. "Sweetheart, you scared me. You became very violent, very quickly. It's not about you being in the right. I'd like you to talk to someone. I don't mean that in an insulting way. I need you to do this for me. I want to be able to help you and I need someone to tell me what's wrong, so I know how."

"I'm not sure I agree with you, Jack. I felt threatened. I felt you were in danger. I needed to act fast and I did."

"I understand, Gracie, and if you want me to shut up, I will. But you knocked the gun away. Instead of going after the gun, you decided to keep pummeling the guy. I'm just worried about you, Gracie. That's all."

One of the officers came out of the room holding up an evidence bag with the gun in it. "Was this the only weapon he had, to your knowledge?"

"It's the only one I saw," Jack responded.

"Okay. Officer Shea is checking the rest of the house. He'll be staying with you until CSU gets here. Neither of you are hurt, right?"

"We're fine," Jack answered.

The officer left and Jack turned back to Gracie. "Do you remember what you were screaming while you were swinging?"

"No. I don't think I was screaming anything. I do remember introducing Matilda, but then I just swung as hard and as fast as I could."

"No, Gracie. You were screaming baseball terms, and your swings were pinpoint-on. Like it was practiced."

"Baseball terms?"

"Yes. Batter up. Hit by the pitch, although you used the word bitch. Foul balls. It scared me."

"I don't remember that," Gracie said, wondering if Jack was making it up. She knew he wouldn't do that.

"Maybe you're right. Maybe I am crazy."

"Don't ever say that again. You're not crazy. But something is wrong, Gracie."

"Okay. I'll check with my sister and see if I have a history. I might know a doctor. If he's still around."

In the morning

Birch

Travis' eyes popped open and he looked over at his phone. Six A.M. What the hell? There was also an alert, so he reached over and picked up the phone, opening the alert.

"Shit!" He rolled out of bed and then apologized to Kris for waking her. He jammed himself into a pair of trousers and darted into the bathroom, splashing water on his face. Then he ran back to the bed, grabbed his phone and dialed Willow.

"Hello? Willow's phone," Mark answered.

"Wake her up," Travis said. "Have her read the alert. Tell her I'm going to go to Community Hospital. Have her check on Jack and Gracie and then meet me there."

"Will do."

Travis continued to make himself as presentable as possible, and once he had his shirt buttoned and tucked in, he grabbed his Nine and the rest of his gear, kissed Kris and made haste to the garage.

Sturgeon

Willow stood at the foot of the bed, dialing her phone. It rang several times before it was finally answered.

"Hello?"

"Grace. This is Detective Sturgeon. Are you guys okay?"

"We're fine. Physically, at least. Jack said I was saying things when I was swinging Matilda, but I don't remember it. These fingerprint people are sure thorough. It looks like it may take them forever. They said he came in through the garage."

"I'm just glad you're safe. I'll jump in the shower and be there as soon as I can."

"Can you bring a bagel or something? They won't let us move from the counter, and Jack and I are a little hungry. They're even in my back yard."

"I have some here. I'll bring a couple and some cream cheese."

"Oh, thank you. We'll see you when you get here."

Mark was being a sweetheart and making the bed, so Willow stripped and jumped into the shower, relating Gracie's request for breakfast. She saw him leave the room. What a man.

Daine

"You'd better have a damn good reason for waking me up, Mrs. Daine."

"I'm so sorry, your honor," Vicki replied. "If I can get you to sign these, we can get into his house and into his computer, and with any luck, find out who hired him."

"You have probable cause that leads you to believe he's the one who killed Arnie?"

"I do. It's in the request. Short version, he broke into a home our witness was staying at. He had a gun with a silencer. I ran him while I was preparing this and he received a traffic citation in Historical yesterday."

"So, what? That officer was bored out of his mind. He's written seven citations in two days. The mayor's been on the captain's case about it."

"He also owns a green Taurus."

The judge looked at her for a long moment and began reading the request. His wife sat a cup of coffee in front of him, smiled at Vicki, and then left the room. Eventually, the judge finished reading and signed the search warrant, handing it back to her.

"I certainly hope if something else comes up, you can find a way to wait until I get to Chambers."

"You're going in? I apologize. I assumed you wouldn't be there, with Thanksgiving and all."

"He's not going in," the wife interrupted, setting buttered toast in front of him. "He just thinks he is."

The judge stared at his wife, thought better of any comment, and looked back at Vicki.

"See what you did?" he directed at her instead. "You can leave."

Vicki thanked the judge, left the home, pushed the button that unlocked her car, and dialed the phone.

Carson

There was something seriously wrong with going into the station this early, but the captain knew this was a critical point in solving the Bayer murder. He sat his coffee and lunch on his desk and took off his jacket just as the phone rang.

"Carson."

"Captain, it's Vicki. I have the search warrant. I'm going to make a call to the Public Defenders' office and then head over to the hospital. I'd bet my career that Birch is there already. I'll give him the warrant."

"Sounds good. And your career is safe. I'll round up whoever's left in CSU and have them meet him at the subject's house at 7:30."

"I'll let him know. I can't let him be there, anyway, until the man's attorney is present."

"Good luck with that," the captain said, hanging up. He picked up the phone again and called the lab.

"Crime Scene Unit, this is Tara."

"Tara, Captain Carson. Who's there with you?"

"Nobody. The whole overnight staff is gone. I'm the first one in."

"They're on an investigation. I need three of you to meet Detective Birch and SWAT at 1213 Cypress at 7:30. This is a complete search-and-recover operation. Especially any computer equipment."

"Okay. I think the truck is still here, if the others didn't take it. Otherwise, we may need a couple of squads."

"You tell me what you need. 7:30 on the dot."

"Got it."

The captain hung up with Tara and called the squad to round up a couple of SWAT members.

Birch

When Travis entered the emergency room, he didn't see any officers. He knew the killer wouldn't be left alone at any time, so he stopped a rushing nurse and asked him where the officer was.

"His prisoner's in X-ray. I'm sure he went with. He was like glue on the guy."

"Which way is that?"

"Basement floor. Right when you come off the elevator."

Travis descended into the basement, and when the elevator doors opened, officer Zahr turned and looked at him, then back through a window. Travis walked up.

"Abe. How's our baby?"

"It's hard not to laugh, Detective, but somehow I've kept it together. This big bad boy got the shit kicked out of him by a five-foot half-pint who can't weigh more than a hundred pounds."

"Yeah? Don't be deceived. There were times during this investigation when she scared me. Has he said anything?"

"Oh, yeah. He has a one-word vocabulary. Lawyer."

"Well. He messed up. I don't think a lawyer's going to get him out of this one."

The officer was silent a moment, and then looked at Travis, saying with sarcasm, "That just hurts me to my core."

"Where to, after the pictures?"

"Back to emergency. The poor guy can't catch a break. No pun intended. The emergency staff don't seem to be in any hurry. Anybody who comes through the door gains priority over the dude. Oh, and they seem to be low on pain meds, too."

"It may seem like that, but that's not the way medical teams work. I'm sure they would just as soon get him out of here as soon as possible."

Zahr snickered with a questionable look. "I don't know about that."

"I know I don't need to tell you; no one talks to him. No one."

"That includes you, ya know. Captain called a few minutes ago. The ADA is on her way, and you're not to question him."

Travis felt the rise in blood pressure. It was a warm feeling in his face, but there was no fuzzy. "What? That's bullshit. I'll find out who hired the guy."

They saw the man being moved across the room, so the two moved into an adjoining room for a better view.

Travis pulled out his tablet. "Give me your notes on his name and address. You guys covered his rights?"

"Shea did. Smith and I witnessed," Zahr said, handing over his own note pad. Travis wrote down the information just as he heard the elevator door open. The click-clack of high heels on the tiled floor caused the two to look at each other.

"Bummer, huh?" Zahr said with a chuckle.

Sturgeon

Willow walked in, handing the bag with the bagels and cheese to Gracie. She and Jack both pulled one out and began applying the cheese. Willow was about to start her questions when her phone dinged. It was a text from Travis.

[Change of plans. We have a warrant. Meet me at 1213 Cypress].

Willow responded that she was on her way. The address sounded familiar. She looked at Gracie scarfing on the bagel and then at Jack, taking a bite but not taking his eyes off Gracie.

"So, what's going on?" she asked. Jack stayed silent. Gracie stopped chewing and hung her head.

"Grace, did you space? It's not uncommon, you know."

"It's not?" Gracie asked, looking a little more self-confident.

"Not at all. Mothers have been known to lift objects off their children that would normally be too heavy for them. Sometimes, weird things happen. It doesn't mean that you are. We have a trauma counselor you can talk to.

She's very good. She can tell you why it happened and what you should do, moving forward."

"How much is that going to cost, do you know? I'm currently unemployed."

"Nothing. Because of your situation, the city foots the bill. What happened, exactly?"

"She was like something out of that suicide squad movie she and I watched one night," Jack said. "She went all Harley Quinn on the guy. Very precise strikes. Knee. Ankle. Wrist. She was screaming at the guy. 'Batter up.' 'Hit by the pitch', although she used bitch. 'Foul balls.' That one I stopped her at, though."

"That's too bad," Willow responded. "I can only imagine the target. I'm sorry I missed it. I liked that movie." Willow looked back and forth between the two, and then continued.

"Listen, guys, I have to talk to the evidence officers and then meet with Detective Birch. Jack, can you stay with Grace until I get arrangements made at the station?"

"I'm not leaving her."

"Good. I'm going to check and see if they need you to stay restricted. I'll be right back."

Birch

Travis reached his vehicle and was about to read the warrant to get the address again when his phone dinged. It was a text from Willow.

[Hey, you. That address you sent me is Carver's neighbor. Albandian, I think his name was].

Travis texted her back, [Yeah. I thought the address looked familiar. See you there.]

Travis loaded the address and left the hospital. His information was that CSU would be there about 7:30. If he didn't run into heavy traffic, that would give him about ten minutes before they kicked him out. He could only hope SWAT would be there early enough. Messing with CSU or entering a potentially dangerous situation without SWAT could get a guy written up.

When he arrived at the neighborhood, he found SWAT sitting at the corner, waiting. He drove to the house and they pulled in behind him. He opened his trunk, pulled his gloves out of the box and, with SWAT in tow, approached the house. SWAT rang the bell and the door was opened immediately by a middle-aged woman. The SWAT officer handed her the warrant and then the two pushed through the door, weapons raised.

The startled woman watched the two progress through the house. She was beginning to cry and show signs of anger. Travis stepped in and spoke to her.

"Mrs. Albandian?"

"Yes. What the hell is wrong with you people? You can't just burst in here like that." Her words were broken due to the fear and tears. Travis was convinced she had no idea who her husband was.

"That paper in your hand says we can," Travis advised. "Can you tell me if your husband has a man cave or a secret area, he's asked you to stay out of?"

"No. What? What the hell is going on? Get those men with guns out of my house. They'll scare the children."

"Clear," one of the officers said as he passed.

"Okay, thanks, guys. Mrs. Albandian . . ." Travis began, but he was interrupted by a woman's voice behind him.

"Good morning, Detective. Excuse us," Tara said as she brushed past him along with two others, each carrying armloads of equipment. They all set their equipment on and around the dining room table, with Tara returning.

Tara looked at Mrs. Albandian and then at Travis, and then back at the woman. "Have you been told why we're here?"

Mrs. Albandian, with her mouth agape and her children holding onto her legs and crying, just stared. Tara looked at Travis.

"Mrs. Albandian," Travis informed her, "I'm afraid your husband has been arrested for a capital crime. It's all explained in the warrant." Travis looked at the children, not wanting to say more.

"Under Carpel city ordinance 1217.3," Tara announced to the woman, "your house is now seized. I'm afraid we'll have to ask you to vacate the premises." Tara didn't wait for acknowledgement. That was Travis' responsibility. Instead, she went back to the dining area and began digging through her cases.

Travis ushered the family outside and asked if there was a friend or relative he could call to pick her up.

"Just get me my car keys from the kitchen counter. I'm going to sue your asses."

"I'm afraid your car is in the garage and considered part of the house. I can call someone for you."

"My God. You people are unbelievable. My phone is on the table. I'll call them myself."

"Once again. . ." Travis said, knowing she would understand her phone was also part of the house.

Mrs. Albandian burst out in tears, no longer able to contain the built-up emotions. She collapsed on the grass, hugging her children to her.

"I've got this, Travis," Willow said from behind him. He nodded, feeling sorry for the woman, and went back into the house. He found Tara measuring the distance between the slider and the hallway, which he found curious, but with her back to him, he turned toward the garage and, as quietly as possible, turned the knob of the garage entrance. "Where are you going, Detective?"

"Just going to see what the garage looks like, Tara."

"Touch nothing. Don't make me kick you out of here."

"Just looking," Travis said. He opened the door and entered the garage. Two cars. One, a white Hyundai SUV, and the other, a green Taurus. He went to the Taurus and looked at the door handle, trying to figure a way to get into the car without Tara throwing a conniption. There didn't seem to be a way. He looked in each window, but didn't see anything helpful.

He moved to the workbench and observed the assorted tools in the same disarray that his own were. There were a good deal of cupboards and hanging tools, none of which he could touch right now. Once CSU was finished, though, he would be touching everything. The one thing Vicki had said before he left the hospital, other than the angry 'Get out' comment, was that there was evidence here. Murderers always left evidence in the one place they thought no one would find. Their home. She told him to find that evidence. He was going to find it.

A CSU officer not named Tara came through the garage door with a camera. "I need the room, please," he announced. Travis walked back to the living area and stood inside, holding the door, while the CSU officer began snapping photo after photo, paying an enormous amount of attention to the Taurus.

After nearly fifty shots, the man walked back toward the interior but stopped at the door. He looked at the slider, the garage, and back at the slider, and then walked back into the garage and out the side door. Travis wasn't sure if he was finished, so he waited. The man came back in, through the garage and past him.

Travis went back inside the garage and back to where he had left off. He was looking for anything out of the norm. He even looked up at the rafters, but found nothing there. He moved to the corner by the garage entrance and looked for anything hanging. Nothing. He was about to move to the opposite corner when the same officer walked back in carrying bolt cutters, walked through and back out the side door. Tool shed?

He followed the man out and watched as the padlock was cut and the door opened. Lawn mower, weed eater, assorted yard items. Nothing spectacular, but the CSU officer began taking photo after photo. Travis left him to it. He went back through the garage and into the house, looking for Willow. He saw her, still outside on the lawn, with Mrs. Albandian. In all likelihood, Willow was at the questioning stage.

He walked over to the table where all of CSU's equipment was, and found several evidence bags already sealed and initialed. Car keys, cell phone. Computer mouse, a paper tablet and a couple of items he couldn't make out.

Tara came out of the back carrying a computer monitor, and she was followed by a man with the tower. He wondered if they even made those anymore, or how old this must be. Tara set the man to wrapping both while she dialed her phone. He eavesdropped.

"Hey, Alex. How close are you guys to being done?" she said into the phone. After a few seconds of response, "Okay, stop by 1213 Cypress. We're going to need the truck." She put the phone back in her pocket and was about to say something to Travis when the Garage Officer came back in.

"Jackpot," he announced as he went back into the garage. Tara followed him, and Travis followed Tara. Through the garage. Out the side door and back to the tool shed, where Travis was looking at the contents of a hidden panel containing nearly twenty different types of firearms, ammunition aplenty, lock pick sets, ski masks, surgical gloves, and best of all? The officer was holding up a journal.

Travis looked at Tara. Tara looked back at him with a smile. "He's toast."

The three of them began scanning the journal. There were dates, two columns with names, two columns with dollar amounts, the first column had a check mark behind most of the names and the second column, likewise, with a couple of exceptions. The column headers were a single letter. D, T, C, R and P. Travis took it to be date, target, client, retainer and payoff. The money columns were pretty hefty.

They paged through the journal and found other writings, and at the back, what looked like a running total and a bunch of gibberish.

"Any idea what any of that says?" Travis asked Tara.

"I speak English, Spanish and French. It's none of those. Swedish, maybe? Swiss? German?"

Travis asked for the journal and went back through it until he found what he was looking for. Almost. Dated three days ago was a line with Bayer's name under the T column. Unfortunately, there was nothing listed under the C column. The R column had 15,000 dollars, and the P column was blank. He handed the journal back to Tara and left the shed. He pulled his phone from his pocket and called the captain.

Sturgeon

It took nearly an hour but Willow finally had Mrs. Albandian and her children calmed down. There was no doubt in her mind, however, that Mr. Albandian had seen the last of them. A friend picked them up. The only friend whose number Mrs. Albandian could remember. Willow did promise the woman that when they had everything they needed, she would call her friend's number and let her know.

Willow still hadn't met up with Travis. She had one more very important call to make. She dialed the number. "This is Dr. Drake. How can I help?"

"Doctor, my name is Detective Willow Sturgeon. I was hoping you could help with a victim of a recent home invasion."

"That's what I'm here for, Willow, and just for future reference, we do away with titles here at the City. My name is Lizzie. I've heard a lot of good things about you from your partner."

"Thank you, Lizzie. I'm at a crime scene right now, so I'll make it brief, if I may."

"Please do."

"We had a killer break into the victim's house to kill another occupant who was a key witness. He was met by the victim. She had a baseball bat and proceeded to thump him pretty good. According to the witness, she was screaming words with each swing, but she has no memory of it." Willow proceeded to tell the doctor the story as it had been related to her, ending with her diagnosis, "Schizophrenia, right?"

"Why, Dr. Sturgeon. How simply wrong of you."

Willow laughed. "Yeah, I should stick to detective work, huh?"

"Yeah, don't quit your day job. What you are describing is Intermittent Explosive Disorder. Rage blackout, to put it simply. That is, if that's all there is to it. It's something I'm very familiar with, naturally, since it's used a lot as an excuse by defense attorneys for bad behavior by their clients when they don't have much else to go on. Why don't you text me her number and I'll give her a buzz and see if we can't set something up."

"Thank you so much, Lizzie. I really like this girl, and I hope you can help her. I'll text you the number. Have a nice day."

"You, too."

Willow sent the number off and then made her way into the house to look for Travis. She found him on the phone, standing over the dining room table, sifting through assorted bags. She reviewed the bags, herself, while waiting for him to finish his call, which appeared to be with the captain.

Travis finished his call and began briefing her on what was found in the tool shed and what he'd found in the garage. Specifically, the green Taurus. Then he went through the items on the table, as well as Tara having found the killer's computer. He also informed her that it sometimes took the hacking team five to six hours to get past the passwords.

"I'm pretty sure I could get Albandian to relinquish those," he announced. "But Vicki won't let me talk to him."

"Really? Why is that, I wonder?"

"This is a big case. She doesn't want any mistakes. She'll be asking the questions herself once the man's public defender gets there. When the captain tells her we have the journal, we'll know who hired him for sure, within minutes."

"I wonder if I can talk Soldier Jack into stopping by and taking a look at that Taurus."

"We can certainly try, but to be honest, I don't think we need it. Keeping that journal was pretty stupid. Vicki will tie him to multiple murders."

"I think he's seen the last of his wife and kids."

"Probably. My guess is he's seen the last of everyone he knows. It depends on what she uses for negotiations. I'm not sure how the death penalty vote went, but California won't execute, in any event. She'll try to use it, though."

"Roughly, how many entries were there?"

"Exactly twenty-two. Including Arnold."

"Yeah. Twenty-two counts of life without the possibility of parole. She'll threaten him with gen-pop, I'll bet."

"I'm not sure. That would give him someone to talk to. She might go solitary without anything other than a toilet and sink. That would suck."

Something else occurred to Willow. What would happen if Mrs. Bayer learned of the arrest? Would she book? Would they have to wait until some officer from some other state made a traffic stop to get her before a judge? "Do you think Mrs. Bayer will flee, if she hears of the arrest?"

"We've got this guy, Will. Even if she flees, we'll eventually find her. There are twenty-one other murders in that journal. This is going to be long and arduous. What we have to do, now, is find anything here that connects him to Mrs. Bayer, and we're home free."

Travis' phone dinged. He read the text and then showed it to her. It was from the captain.

[Crocket got the guy on a traffic ticket in Historical. Units looking for second car near original scene. Will advise.]

Three other CSU officers came through the front door and asked where Tara was. Travis directed them to the garage and they left that direction in unison.

With the same CSU officers who had been at Gracie's now here, Willow assumed they were done there, so she excused herself from Travis and stepped away to call Gracie.

"Hello?"

"Hi, Grace, this is Detective Sturgeon. Did you get a call from Dr. Drake?"

"No. Who's he?"

"She. Our department's crisis counselor. She'll be calling you soon. She told me what you went through. Is it possible to talk to Jack for a second?"

"Sure, hang on," Grace responded, and then Jack came on. "Yes?"

"Jack, we found a green Taurus at the guy's house. Would you be able to identify it as the car you saw leaving Historical?"

"Maybe. A Taurus is about the right size. I may have to look at it from a distance."

"Okay. I'll talk to CSU and see if they've processed it yet. I'll call you back."

Willow went back to Travis. "I take it Tara's in charge?"

"That would be my guess," Travis said. "She's been pretty bossy."

Willow went the direction the others had gone but found no one in the garage. She did see the Taurus, and even knowing there was nothing for her to see, she fell to the temptation of looking inside anyway.

She walked out the side door and found everyone staring wide-eyed at the arsenal, with Tara and one other sitting inside, logging serial numbers and tagging weapons. She was about to ask Tara to process the Taurus when the woman's cell phone started playing a ringtone of "Don't Touch That" by Group X. Willow laughed louder than she intended, causing everyone to look at her.

Tara finished her call and then asked those present, "Who has a car?"

No one answered, so she asked one of the men to take over for Laticia. The man took off toward the inside of the home and Willow took the opportunity. "Tara, is it possible to back the Taurus out of the garage? I have a witness coming over, and he has to see it at a distance."

"Roger, process the Taurus, please. The keys are on the kitchen table."

Willow called Jack back, asking him to come and look, while another man left for the inside and a woman came out asking Tara where she was needed.

"They found the second car at the Walmart parking lot near the first scene. I need it processed. There's a cell phone inside. I need that, too."

Willow nearly yelped. "Can we look at that phone before it's tagged?"

"Sure. After Laticia is done with it."

Willow darted inside and found Travis nearly in the same spot. "They found the second car, Travis. Albandian's phone is inside."

"Are we going to have access?"

"Tara told the tech to bring it back here. Do we want to wait? She said we could look at it after the tech was finished. We could go there and ask her to do that first."

"We will if we need to. The killer is in custody. I've just heard from Vicki. There are two officers at the hospital and there will continue to be, until he's healed enough for transfer. There's stuff here I still want to look at."

"Okay. Jack's on his way to look at the Taurus."

"Good. While you're waiting, see if they're finished with the master bedroom. If they are, tear it apart. There's no Mantle card on this table. It's either here, in a storage unit, or a bank safe deposit box. That's your focus, for now."

Daine

Vicki sat at the table, waiting for the public defender to finish looking over the evidence against his client. She was patient and provided him all the time he needed to come at her with anything he thought he could argue. She knew he had nothing, and no amount of reviewing the evidence was going to provide him with anything. She had Albandian by the short hairs and she knew the public defender would realize that.

"Shee-it," the public defender announced, in his somewhat unprofessional manner. "This guy doesn't need an attorney. He needs God to perform a miracle."

"I appreciate your honesty, Mr. Fleming," Vicki replied. "Should we get down to business, or do you need more time?"

"What do you need from him and what would be his incentive?"

"It costs the State of California $90,000 per year to house a death-row inmate. It only costs $47,000 to house in gen-pop. It benefits us to house him in gen-pop, and that will be twenty-two counts of life, without. I will ask the judge and warden to deny him any luxuries and we can cut that cost to about $30,000. The man should be so lucky to receive the death penalty, but it is my intention to make his twenty-two lives as miserable as possible.

"I want to know who hired him to kill Arnold Bayer. If he gives me that and testifies, I'll not use my influence against him. There's nothing else I need from him, and I'll be honest with you, he doesn't have a lot of time to decide. The detectives on this case are very good. They'll find out who hired him. They already have a person of interest. If they find out before he tells me, the offer's off the table."

Fleming hesitated, then responded, "That death penalty thing isn't going to work for you guys anymore, you know? It's no secret that California wouldn't enforce a death verdict if someone killed every judge in the state. There is no longer a fear of it. I can guarantee he already knows that. I'm not trying to be difficult, Counselor. I'm just stating fact. I'll go to him with your offer, if that's the best you've got, but I don't believe he'll think you have the influence to uphold the threat."

"I'm not saying this happens, of course, but it's always possible that there is a backscratching situation going on. As an example, suppose the warden of a particular prison needed help at a parole hearing for someone who was reformed and born again. That help would be provided and the warden would then 'owe a favor'. Of course, that's all hypothetical."

Fleming smiled. "I see your point. Hypothetically, of course, and I'm guessing the hypothetical judge influence would be of a similar nature."

Vicki just shrugged. "You don't have a lot of time, Counselor. Shouldn't you be on your way to the hospital?" Fleming stood.

"I'll present your offer. I'm not sure how much he knows, or if he'll buy in, but I'll get back to you as soon as I can."

"I've already been there this morning. He knows what he faces. He just doesn't know about what we've already found. His hidden compartment. His journal. His second car. His phone. He needs to decide fast."

Fleming nodded and left. Vicki loaded her messages on her phone. Still no word from CSU on the weapons. There must be a lot of them, or she would have info by now. She needed to contact the assorted cities on the list from the journal but she needed calibers first. The out-of-town murders would be unsolved, naturally, or Albandian would already be in prison. She needed as much info as possible to give to the assorted cities in order to connect him to the murders.

One of the murders was local, and she had already found it had been cold-cased. GPS info and whichever weapon he used would tie him to that murder. She would have to wait until the file arrived to make the connection.

The first of her assistants finally came back, and she set him to the task of calling the various cities in the journal to prep them for her later call. He was to give them the murder victim's name and the client's name only, for now. She just didn't have much more to offer at this time.

Vicki wasn't kidding herself. There was no way she was prosecuting this man. One of the murders was in Oregon, and one was in Utah. Her boss would be calling her by the end of the day, informing her that federal prosecutors would be taking over. She knew that. That was why she'd told Fleming he needed to hurry. She wanted the person who'd hired Albandian.

Fleming knew she would lose the case, too. He was just not saying so because he, himself, would need a favor at some point. He knew this was a lost cause. No one alive could get this man off. He would do his job, because that was his job, but he wasn't a fool.

Vicki wanted to make certain it was a high-profile case with a lot of media coverage. It would discourage future murder-for-hire attempts, for one thing. For another, she had dreams and aspirations, just like everyone else. It never hurt the resume to get a conviction like this. Regardless of whether or not she was able to try the man, the Feds couldn't take the person who'd hired him. That case would be hers.

Another assistant came in and told her there was a call for her on line one. She picked up the receiver. It was the captain.

"Good morning, again, Counselor," the captain greeted. "I was hoping I could use your name for an order to the field."

"Probably. Explain."

"I've just received a call from the CSU head at one of the scenes. One of her people, processing the second car, found some disturbing photos on your man's phone while pairing it. They're photos of the inside of Birch's house. It's not something I want Birch to know, right now. I don't think he would do anything rash, but eliminating the temptation would assure it."

"How's this? I need the chain of custody on that phone to be a bare minimum for trial. It is to be brought to me. Sealed."

"Perfect. Thanks for your help."

Boy, Vicki thought, this guy is a real piece of work. Breaking into a cop's house. Cocky bastard. That could have been a real nut cruncher if he had been caught. She began typing again on her computer, adding another case of home invasion to the charges. She picked up her phone and dialed.

"This is Tara."

"Tara, this is ADA Daine. I know you don't need added pressure in cases like this, but I really need you to find something, anything, that indicates who hired him. Do you have anyone available who can begin digging into his computer?"

"I can dig someone up. It will take a bit to bypass passwords, though. I'll get someone on it, right away."

"Thank you, Tara."

Before she could even hang up, another call beeped in. It was Fleming.

"This is ADA Daine," she answered.

"Well, I gave him the list of charges and told him about your offer. He said he will give you the name of the person who hired him if you drop the murder charge to manslaughter and destroy the journal."

"What the hell, Fleming? Why are you even calling me with that? That's not going to happen. In fact, I've just added another charge. We found photographs of the interior of a Carpel detective's home on his phone. You can add the fact that I will stop adding charges to my previous offer if he points her out in a line-up."

"Her?"

"That's right, Fleming. We already know who hired him. We want her to go away for a long time. He makes that happen and it will go easier on him. I'll tell the judge of his cooperation."

"You want me to tell him the judge isn't going to give a shit about his cooperation, or keep that to myself?"

"You decide. You won't be having a relationship with him once he's convicted, but you and I will see each other a lot on future cases, so tell him what you think is best. I'm loaded and I'm coming after him with all the nastiness I can muster."

"Calm down, Daine. I'm not the killer."

"Nope. Not calming down. You have my offer. There will be no further negotiation on the matter. You call me with an agreement to attend a line-up, or I'll see you in court. Have a nice rest of your day." Vicki didn't wait for acknowledgement. She hung up her phone.

Sturgeon

The tech that Tara had assigned to the Taurus was cleaning up his mess and Willow was standing at the front, waiting. Once he was done, she would back the car out of the garage to wait for Jack, and then the tech would be working on the floor of the garage where the Taurus had sat. That couldn't possibly take long. It was probably just a quick view of the eye. He had told her he could do the thorough search with the car outside. She would be allowed to help with that and she was eager to do so. She still hadn't found the Mantle card.

He gave her the nod and she climbed in and started the engine. It started right away and sounded smooth. It was a good working vehicle. She backed it out of the garage and popped the trunk. She looked forward and saw the tech was indeed just eyeing the garage floor. She couldn't imagine what he would be looking for, so she asked.

"Shavings," the man said. And that was all he said. *Thanks for the info* was what Willow felt like saying, but she dropped the subject and went back to the trunk. She began pulling at the side walls and seat backs but nothing moved. She pulled the floor cover up and checked the underside, and there it was. A heavily wrapped in cellophane bag containing a small card with a baseball player on it that she assumed was Mickey Mantle. Fifty-thousand-dollars, huh? It was taped to the underside of the cover.

She was about to ask the tech to dust the cellophane when she noticed a car stopped at the end of the street. She closed the trunk and car door and carried the floor cover into the garage, setting it on the hood of the SUV.

The tech was about to start with the car but she stopped him and asked him to print the card instead. He went for his case and Willow leaned against the garage door, staring out at Jack, giving him as much time as possible to be sure. After nearly a minute, Jack began walking toward her, much to the dismay of Gracie, who was throwing her arms up in the air and stomping her feet. She eventually just got back in her car and drove to where Willow was.

When she arrived, she stormed out of her car and approached Willow with an angry face. "Ooh, that man. He just walks away without a word."

Willow smiled. "Good thing he doesn't live with you, huh?"

Gracie's face lit up with recognition. "Oh my God. He did that on purpose."

Willow patted her shoulder and the two just watched as Jack neared the house. "Maybe just give it a break for a bit, Grace. Don't talk about it for a time. Then just invite him to dinner. Be slow and deliberate. Maybe you're just coming on too strong for him."

"I'll try it. At this point, I'll try anything. That doctor called me. I go in Monday."

"Good. That's pretty quick. She must be bored."

"No. She read off many options, some of which were over a month away. I just took the earliest one."

"You'll like her, I think. Travis said she's very good and very nice. He also said she's not someone you can lie to. She reads people well."

"How does he know that? Lies a lot, does he?"

"All cops will, Grace. If they think she's not going to let them return to work."

"That's just wrong," Gracie finished. Willow was about to respond but Jack was walking up the driveway.

"I'm not sure how much my testimony is going to help, Detective," Jack announced when he reached them. "I can say that it's the right size and the right color, but that's about it. The guy even shaved off his goatee."

"One of the techs found his goatee in the garbage, Jack," Willow said. "And even if your testimony isn't needed, you've helped a great deal in this investigation. I think we have enough, even without the car. According to the captain, the ADA is salivating."

"So! I can go back to Historical, then?"

Gracie's eyes bulged and Willow caught it. "I can't advise that quite yet, Jack. Although he is in custody, we are not yet totally satisfied he worked alone. Soon, though.

What are the odds of getting you to spend Thanksgiving weekend with Grace? If for no other reason, I'm sure she could use some help cleaning up our mess."

"Please, Jack," Gracie added. "You could help me cook a turkey. We can stop at the store on the way back." Jack looked at Gracie, at Willow, and then back at Gracie. "Fine. I haven't seen this kind of conspiracy in nearly forty years. If you're going to gang up on me like that, I suppose I have no choice."

Gracie grabbed Jack's arm in a hug, placing her head on his shoulder. "You won't regret it, Jack. I'm an excellent cook."

Jack patted her arm. "I know, Gracie. I've already tasted it. Let's go, then."

Willow watched the two as they walked toward the car and smiled. Then, turning, she grabbed the Taurus trunk cover and walked into where Travis was still sifting through the CSU finds on the table.

"Hey, Travis. Look what I found."

"Oh, man. Another nail in the coffin. That's proof he was the burglar who stole the murder weapon." Travis looked around at all the techs digging, dusting and hauling. Willow followed his eyes, knowing he wanted someone to check for prints on the cellophane but there didn't appear to be anyone that wasn't elbows-deep. It was too much fun not telling him she had already had it dusted. She notified Travis that she would check with Tara. Then she leaned the trunk cover against the table and went back through the garage. She found Tara still in the shed and still logging weapons, only about half-way through.

"Hey, Tara. We found the Mantle card. It was wrapped in cellophane and taped to the underside of the trunk cover of the Taurus. Travis will probably ask you to print it. I already had that done, so feel free to tell Travis you'll get around to it. It is proof that our man was the one who broke into Carver's house."

Tara seemed indifferent to the news or the humor and practical joke, but the man helping her looked like he was about to jump out of his shoes. "I can check that real quick, T," he said.

Tara just shook her head with a smirk. "Go ahead. You look like you're about to have a coronary. Look at the card, dust it again, bag it, take a picture and get back here. I don't want to be at this all day."

The man sat his pad down and darted past Willow. Willow took the opportunity to check on another item. "Any word from the tech at the car yet? That phone has things we need for our report."

"That's not going to happen, Detective. Sorry. We have orders from ADA Daine. She wants that phone delivered to her, untouched by anyone other than Laticia."

"Why? Did she say?"

"She did not. The orders were relayed through the captain. You might want to ask him."

"Thanks. I will." Willow left the shed and went back through the garage to Travis. The tech that absolutely needed an excuse to be able to put his eyes on the Mantle card had the trunk cover flat against the floor and was dusting the cellophane. She gave her partner the news about the phone.

"What the hell?" he blurted and immediately began dialing his phone.

Birch

"Carson."

"What the hell, Cap?" Travis asked. "What possible reason could there be that we wouldn't have access to the man's phone? We need his contact information and pictures he may have taken. Especially if one of those pictures are of a particular client."

"No, you don't," the captain retorted. "If there are any pictures of Mrs. Bayer on the phone, the ADA will send her own people out to nab her. Arnie is not his only victim, and the ADA doesn't want anyone responsible for that phone except her."

"Bullshit. She has the damn journal. She can just pair the damn thing. I have no problem going to her office and doing it myself. I'll call her."

"No, Birch. You won't. Let's not forget who's in charge here. I want you to find everything you can at that house that might connect him to Arnie's wife. If there's anything on that phone that helps us, she'll call me and I'll let you know. I'm sure it won't be a problem allowing you to assist in the arrest."

"Oh. I'm so honored," Travis spat sarcastically. "You need to talk to her, Cap. We need to see that phone. Even if we have to go to her office to do it."

"You have your orders. I'm done talking about this. Find something in that house. There has to be something there. Get to work. While I have you on the phone, let Tara know that Mrs. Albandian's attorney brought by a court order demanding the release of the SUV and her cell phone." Before Travis could respond again, the captain hung up.

Travis shoved his phone back in his pocket none too gently. His mind was awhirl. There was something on that phone that either the captain or the ADA considered top secret. Something that either he, or Willow, shouldn't or couldn't be allowed to see. *ADA only, my ass!*

It would be a while before his mind cleared of the phone fiasco, but he went back to the items on the table anyway. He noticed Willow's look of concern and guessed she could see his anger.

"We're not getting access to the phone," he announced. "The reason I was given is bullshit. There's no such thing as withholding evidence in a murder investigation by the ADA. There's something on that phone that either you or I are not allowed to see."

Willow joined him at the table, sifting through evidence bags in trying to find something that said 'Mrs. Bayer'. The Mantle card had shifted their focus. That card had proved that Albandian had been in possession of the Garcia. He had been the one who had entered Carver's domain and stolen the valuables. Now, their focus was on finding a connection to Mrs. Bayer.

As he was pushing bags aside, he noticed Willow was only half present. She was looking, but she was also thinking.

"Let's have it," he said to her.

"Have what?"

"Don't give me that. You have a thought about the phone. I want to hear it."

"Even if I did, which I didn't, it would be purely theoretical. What have you told me about theories?"

Travis stopped with the evidence bags and just stared at her. "You have an idea. I can tell by that expression. What is it?"

"You're crazy. I don't have any ideas about the phone. I wish I did. I'd like to see what his contacts look like. I was actually thinking about what my chances were of getting out of here with that Mantle card."

Travis continued to stare at her, not believing her for a second, but he also knew she couldn't be intimidated into revealing her thoughts. He would have to dig it out of her in stages. Before he went back to the evidence bags, he walked through the garage and let Tara know about the SUV and Mrs. Albandian's cell phone. He walked back through the garage just in time to see Willow sticking her phone back in her pocket. Yeah, she suspected something.

He went back to the table and began, once again, checking bags for anything that would connect Albandian to Mrs. Bayer. He caught himself several times pushing bags around but not looking at their contents, his mind on the contents of Albandian's phone instead.

"I think I'm going to head out, Will," he announced. "I'm going to go see the captain and maybe Vicki, if she's in the office."

"Okay. I can finish up here. If there's anything that connects the two, I'll call you."

Travis started for the door, then turned. "Unless there's something you want to tell me."

Willow continued to sift, not even looking at him. "I've got nothing for you, Travis. I wish I did. I'd like to know what's on that phone, myself."

Travis suddenly was unsure if Willow knew anything or not. He suspected she did but she was acting and talking like she didn't. He didn't want to be paranoid but he had a strange feeling that there was something on that phone that he wasn't supposed to see. If that son of a bitch had taken pictures of his wife or kids, he might not make trial.

He left the house and deliberately drove the direction of Albandian's car. He was too late. The tech was gone and the car was being hoisted onto a tow truck. Travis increased his speed. He had a change of plans. He was going to see Vicki first. Maybe he could cut the tech off.

He took every shortcut he could think of but it still took him fifteen minutes to reach the DA's office. He found a spot on the ramp to park and hurried to the elevator.

When the door to the lobby opened, he saw the tech from Albandian's house standing at the desk of the ADA's secretary. He stayed calm, but walked over to confront the tech.

"Hey, how are you?" he asked. "I'm sorry, I didn't get your name. I'm Detective Birch, with homicide." Travis stuck out his hand.

"Officer Laticia Anderson," the woman responded, shaking his hand.

Travis spoke quickly, "I'm working the Albandian case. Can I see that bag for just a second?" He reached for the evidence bag with the phone. Laticia pulled the bag back.

"I'm sorry, Detective. My orders are crystal-clear. It doesn't leave my hands until I hand it, personally, to ADA Daine."

"No problem," Travis said. "You can hold on to it. Just turn it so we can see through the bag and activate the Photo app."

"Hey, Birch," a man said, with his hand pulling Travis back by the arm. Travis recognized the man as one of the ADA's investigators. Travis shook the hand off his arm and pointed at the phone, looking at Laticia. The man grabbed his arm a second time and put his hand on Travis' chest, pushing him away from the tech.

Travis shook the man's hands off and pushed him against the secretary's desk, holding him there. "You put your hands on me again and we're going to have a serious problem."

The investigator wasn't intimidated. He grabbed Travis' chin and squeezed his cheeks together, pushing him back. Travis was about to counter, when he heard the loud command.

"DEE-TECK-TIVE," Vicki said with volition. "You will remove yourself from my offices, immediately. I hope you don't think you are above prosecution for hindering my investigation and contaminating evidence." She put her hand on the investigator's arm. "Let him go, Jerry."

The investigator released his grip on Travis' chin and Travis reciprocated. He turned on Vicki. "Are you going to tell me what's on that phone that I'm not supposed to see, Vicki?"

Vicki walked over to the tech and accepted the evidence bag, "Thank you, officer. This is all I needed. You can go back to whatever fun you were having." Then she turned toward Travis.

"It's Counselor Daine, Detective," she said acidly, "and I told you to leave." She pointed at her secretary, and the secretary began dialing her phone. Vicki began walking back to her office, with the investigator following. Travis was not done.

"Are there pictures of my wife and kids on that phone?" he asked, following the two.

Vicki ignored him and continued to walk. His phone dinged. When he looked, he saw it was a text from the captain.

[Get here. Now. This minute.]

Vicki and the investigator entered her office and closed the door, leaving him on the outside, looking in. He contemplated walking in, but he decided to take his grievance up with the captain.

Daine

"Where was I?" Vicki asked.

"Find where the sister lives," Jerry answered.

"Yeah. When you find that, sit on her. If you need help, let me know and I'll get the department to loan me a couple uniforms. If she goes to the airport, train station or bus depot, detain her."

"What reason do we give her, or is that our problem?"

"Wanted for questioning," Vicki answered. She stuck the evidence bag in her desk drawer and locked the drawer. "This is going to mess up Thanksgiving for you guys. I'm sorry about that but she can't leave town. If she does, it would take too much manipulation to get her back."

"It would be nice if we could shut down the city during holidays, but for some reason that request hasn't gone over too well. We'll survive."

"I'll do everything I can to help. If I knew for absolute certainty that she was the one who hired this guy, I would just say bring her in and ruin her holiday, instead of ours. There is, however, an element of doubt."

Jerry stood. "We do what we need to, Vic. That's what you pay us for. I'm going to get started. Anything else?"

"No. That's it," Vicki said. As Jerry reached the door, she felt the need to reinforce her gratitude. "And Jerry. Thanks for all you do. Thank Alan for me, too." Jerry nodded and left just as her secretary informed her of a pending call. Fleming.

"I hope you're not calling with another insulting offer," she answered without a hello.

"Nope. It was difficult to convince him that angels from heaven couldn't get him off, but once I explained how the justice system works and that even twelve jurors passed out on meth would still find him guilty, he finally saw the light.

"However," Fleming continued, "he still doesn't trust that you have the pull you say you do. He wants me to get it in writing, signed by you, a judge and the warden."

"No deal. I'll write it up and sign it and I'll have the warden and a few others at the prison sign it but there's no way I'm getting a judge to commit to something he has no control over."

"That will work. I already told him you wouldn't agree to the judge part. I'll be over this afternoon to pick it up. Is that enough time?"

"Plenty," Vicki responded. "I'll have it drawn up now, sign it, make the call to the warden and have it taken out for his signature. It should be back here by two or three this afternoon."

"Sounds good. See you then."

Vicki hung up the phone and punched her intercom. "Sheri, get everybody in here, pronto."

"Yes, ma'am," came the response.

Within minutes, her office chairs were filled with all three interns and her secretary. She pulled the killer's phone from her desk, greeted each, made sure they all brought in their notepads and pen, and began.

"Sheri, I need a document with the usual flair, on letterhead, with the details I have in my notes marked Bayer case. There needs to be a signature space for my name, warden James Quall, and two other signature lines. In exchange for testifying for the prosecution and attending a suspect line-up, this office extends the following amenities. And then list what I have on the notes.

"Ben," Vicki switched, "when she has that finished, I need you to run it out to the prison and have the warden and a couple of his assistants sign it. Call first, though, to make sure he hasn't left early for the holiday.

"Dave," she continued, holding the bagged phone out, "I need you to pair this and search for any notes, documents, photos or anything else, using the keywords: Carpel, client, Birch, target and fee." Dave accepted the bag.

"Cora, I need you to drive over to the crime scene and touch base with Tara. You're looking for a completed list of the weapons found, his journal and anything she has found with the name Arnold Bayer on it. Just like Ben, call first to make sure they haven't cleared out. When you get back, start digging into unsolved murders and try to find a correlation. The rest of you will help her, when you finish your tasks."

Vicki clapped her hands a couple times. "Let's get this done, so we can enjoy our Thanksgiving."

With everyone filing out, Vicki opened the photo app on her phone to the man's journal entries and began writing down victim names and cities. She was very appreciative of the speed and precision of Tara, getting these photos to her so quickly. These entries could be unsolved murders, falsely accused killers, missing persons or any number of other cases.

The cities involved could be those handling the cases, or it could be adjoining cities, or suburbs, or in some cases the city in which the victim went missing. This was going to be a long process, tying each name to its respective open or cold case.

With some of the names, it would just be providing the families with closure. With some, it would just be a matter of closing cases. She would intentionally do the out-of-state cases last, to give her as much time as possible to find and arrest the woman who had hired Albandian. This afternoon, she would begin preparing her statement for the media. In all likelihood, she wouldn't be able to get her name and face in the news. The boss would probably issue the statement. He had ambitions, too. She had every intention of being prepared, just in case.

Birch

Travis had a bone to pick, and it may as well be with the captain. Entirely too many people were trying to keep him away from Albandian's phone. He could only think of one reason. The man had photos that were going to set Travis off.

It looked like the majority of the department had already left for the holiday. There were plenty of parking spots. CSU was straggled throughout the city, as well, which opened a few more. He chose the closest to the door he could find and began climbing the concrete steps into the department.

When he reached the detective bureau, the captain was standing in his doorway, looking none too happy. And that look of unhappiness was staring at Travis. He just pointed at Travis and then turned the finger to the interior of his office. Travis obliged.

"He put his hands on me and was pushing me, Cap. It was just a misunderstanding. All is good."

"No, Birch," the captain countered. "All is not good. You're taking the rest of the holiday off. I don't want you talking to Daine, Albandian, Sturgeon or any member of CSU for the next four days."

Travis was stunned and he was sure his face showed it. He regained himself. "What the hell for, Captain? I still have things to do at that house."

"Sturgeon can handle it. I've sent a squad over to partner with her for the rest of the day. Since you've become so adept at disregarding my wishes, it's obvious to me you need time to rethink your position with the department. I'm not removing you from the case, at this time, but that will be my next step if things don't change.

"Perhaps I have been too lenient over the years. If that's the case then this is all my fault. I'm correcting that now. I gave you a direct order and you disobeyed it. Normally, that would be grounds for suspension. Consider yourself fortunate that it's Thanksgiving. Go home. Spend the four days with the family and come back here Monday, refreshed and considerably wiser."

Travis sat with his thumb and forefinger resting against his chin, staring down the captain. "Are there pictures of my wife and kids on that phone, Captain?"

"No. And yet that is another question about the case, despite what I've just told you. You are pushing the envelope way too far, Birch. Go. Home. Now. Right now. Before I am forced to make it disciplinary."

Travis wasn't sure he believed the answer, but that was obviously the only answer he was going to get and the one he was going to have to live with. He wasn't done. He was a detective, and his instincts told him to begin a hard grilling of the man across the desk, but he also knew that man could strip him of the only job he had ever held. Before he said something he would regret, he stood and walked out the door.

He didn't bother wishing the captain a happy Thanksgiving. It was pretty childish of him, and he would need to apologize later. He had learned long ago that counting to ten didn't always work. Sometimes the best course of action was to simply walk away. He didn't think anyone going into their holiday needed to be subjected to his current mood.

Getting into his car and driving home, he would have to clear his mind of the incident. It wasn't Kris' fault, and it certainly wasn't that of the kids. He didn't want to take it out on them. He had no intention of doing so. He began thinking positive thoughts about the holiday and using those thoughts to prod deep into his memories.

The memory of his brother joining them for turkey dinner. The memory of the time he had done all the cooking and preparation, and the secrecy involved, and the assistance of one of Kris' friends to get her out of the house so he could do so. He realized he was laughing inside the car at that memory.

His thoughts were interrupted by his phone. It was Pete. Answering it would probably ruin his mood again. On the other hand, Pete had worked hard at whatever he had found that prompted the call. There was a way out. He keyed the sync.

"Birch."

"Hey, Birch. I have information for you from that search you sent me on."

"That's great, Pete. I'm driving and can't stop to make notes right now. Can you do me a favor and call Will? She's at the killer's house and can write it down for me."

"Sure will. Going to be heading home in a few. Happy Thanksgiving."

"To you and the family as well, Pete, and thank you for all you do." Travis keyed the off button and went back to his pleasant memories. Picnics in the park. Trips to the beach. The huge eyes of the kids when they open their Christmas presents. Fixing Macy's favorite doll. Teaching Ashton how to fish. His memories were working so well that he was home in no time.

He opened the garage door and saw the kids running around in the yard, playing two-person tag. He tried to decide how much fun two-person tag could possibly be. Then two of the neighbor's kids came into view, one of which was 'it'. Kris was inside the garage, moving clothes from the washer to the dryer. He wondered how long it would take her to remind him of his promise to move the two machines inside. He pulled in and shut the engine off.

"What's going on? Why are you home so early?" Kris asked.

"Through the kindness of the captain," Travis answered.

Kris glared at him with a questionable look as she shook out a shirt. "You're not taking advantage of Willow, are you? Making her finish up while you come home?"

"Not at all," Travis said as he kissed his wife. "She may be on her way home, too. I was at the station. She was at one of the scenes."

Kris gave him that sideways glance. The one she always used just before she reamed him a new one. What the hell was it about women? Would he ever figure out how they knew they were being lied to?

"Okay," Travis said, "the captain and I got into a disagreement and he told me to go home and calm down."

"About what?" Kris asked, now not even looking at him while she separated the laundry.

"My ability to have access to certain evidence. All's good. I'm home. I thought you'd be happier about that than you are."

Kris turned to him and planted a kiss on him. "I am happy, honey. Sorry I'm so inquisitive. Are you going to help me prep for tomorrow's dinner, or move the washer and dryer inside the house?"

Travis couldn't help but laugh. That was less than five minutes. "I'll do both, but the washer and dryer will have to wait until after the holiday."

"Which holiday?"

"You're not going to let up, are you?"

"Which holiday?" Kris repeated.

"I'll work on it this weekend. Do we have any other obligations other than Willow and Mark?"

"No. I'll wake you up early on Friday, so you can go to Lowe's and get your supplies."

Travis was about to object, but there was that look again, daring him. He ran things through his head, trying to come up with the best response that would avoid him having to get up early. He decided on the only workable solution.

"Okay. Sounds good."

Sturgeon

Her phone only rang once. She didn't even look, thinking it was Travis. It wasn't. "Sturgeon."

"Hey, Will. Birch was driving. He told me to call you."

"What's up, Petey?"

"Well. First of all, never call me Petey again. Secondly, it took some serious digging, having to go through all the redirects, but I found your man. He's a snake."

"I hope you didn't make me stop what I was doing and answer my phone for that tidbit of news."

"No. His code name that he uses for client contact is Ophidian. There are several entries here, Will. It looks like he's been a busy boy."

"Yeah, we have his journal. Twenty-two, I think it was."

"Try thirty-seven. There doesn't seem to be a way to determine which are complete, which he may have turned down or which may be pending. Obviously, if there are twenty-two complete, then there are fifteen unaccounted for. Which means some he may have been hired for, but aren't yet killed. One of those is Barack

Obama, which he naturally would have turned down. That still leaves fourteen or so."

"Is there contact information on all of them? Real names?"

"There's no way to know if the names are real, but yeah, there are names. Otherwise, he wouldn't know who to talk to for the payoff."

"What's the name listed with Arnold Bayer?"

"Unfortunately, they're all just first names. No last names. The name listed at the end of the email about Arnie is Barbara."

"That's the wife. Great work. I'll take it from here. Thanks, Petey."

"Dammit, Will. . ."

Willow stuck her phone back in her pocket and pulled out her notepad, made all the notes she could remember about her conversations and interviews that were in any way related to Mrs. Bayer. She would need to refer to those notes when she called the captain. She tried to anticipate his every question. When she had noted everything she could think of, she pulled the phone from her pocket.

"Detective Sturgeon?" the uniformed officer asked before she could dial.

"Yes?"

"I'm Officer Sims. The sarge asked me to come and assist where I could. He said if you had questions, you should call the captain."

Willow stuck out her hand, introducing herself, and the officer accepted it. She was absolutely going to call the captain. First, though, she wanted to know how it was she didn't know this man.

"We haven't seen each other, have we? I'm sorry, I don't recognize you."

"I'm one of the new hires. Feel free to tag me with whatever the latest craze is."

Willow laughed. "No. I won't be doing that. A first name would be nice, though."

"Stanley. Or Stan, to most."

"Okay, Stan it is. What I would like you to do is check the back yard for any areas that look like something might be buried or hidden. Don't dig or even scratch. If you see something that is questionable, contact Tara. She is in the shed, logging weapons, right now. She's in charge of this operation. If you don't find anything, come on back. You can help me with this sorting."

Stan nodded and exited through the slider. As soon as he was out the door, she pulled out her phone and called the captain. She was more than a little concerned with why she had a tag-along. Where was Travis? Before she could hit send, another number was calling in. It was Travis' house phone.

"Kris?"

"Nope. It's me," Travis answered. "I got into a little hot water and have been sent home with a note attached to my chest. I can't be involved in the case over the weekend."

"Okay, then I won't tell you that Pete found the guy on the web and that his code name is Ophidian and that his contact for the Bayer hit was Barbara."

"That's the wife's name, right?" Travis asked, with a little venom in his voice.

"Yup. I'm about to call the captain, and go pick her up and ruin her holiday."

"Well, you can call the captain, but I'll bet you won't be picking her up."

"Why the hell not?"

"Because, Willow. That Miranda bitch has taken over. Before I left there, she sent her investigators to sit on the wife. She would love nothing more than to arrest her and let her guys enjoy Thanksgiving."

"Okay. That's fine. As long as she's arrested before she can skip."

"Dammit, Willow. Why are you such a pussy about this? You were okay with the FBI taking over the last case, and now this. It's our case. Our collar."

"Did you just call me a pussy, you dick? Collar? Our case? This isn't the twentieth century, Travis. It's about arrest and conviction. Not personal goals."

"Tell that to Miranda."

Willow was about to respond but Travis hung up on her without even a goodbye. Now, she was the one who was pissed. She called him back. Kris was the one who answered.

"He hung up on me. The bastard. Did he run and hide?"

'He's in the bathroom, so I would say yes," Kris said. "Dinner's at one tomorrow. Bring your nightstick. The kids and I will hold him down for you."

"Uhh," Willow dragged out, "okay. I'll see you tomorrow."

Willow was about to call the captain, but once again was interrupted. This time by Stan. She had a sudden thought. If she didn't tell the captain, she and Stan could save everybody a lot of time by going and picking up the woman themselves. Of course, that wouldn't work. Travis had said that the ADA's people were sitting on her. Not only that, but she had just told Travis that it wasn't about personal goals.

"Find anything?" she asked Stan.

"Nah, it just looks like a yard. There are a few toys, but they looked harmless. I was going to go through the trash bins, but thought I'd better ask Tara first. I did. She said, and I quote, 'Hands off'."

"Yeah. They're pretty strict about what we can and can't touch. Okay, what I'm looking for here is anything that might connect the killer to the victim or the victim's wife. These, I've already gone through," she said, pointing at a set of bags on one end of the table. "We need to get through the rest of these, and we can touch all we want because they're in evidence bags. The guys will keep bringing stuff as they find it, so it's pretty unending. The victim's name is Arnold Bayer, and the wife's name is Barbara. You start at the end, down there. I'll work my way to you."

"Got it," Stan said, as he began inspecting.

Things were starting to come to an end in the case, Willow thought. Just as she thought it, that annoying voice that always sounded a lot like Travis reminded her that it wasn't over until it was over. Barbara would be enough to get a jury to convict, but a wise attorney could beat that with the proper arguments.

Willow knew there would be a line-up, and Albandian, or Ophidian, or whatever name he chose, would be asked to pick her out. That would be the clincher, not the name Barbara. Willow pulled her phone out again and called the captain.

"Carson," he answered.

"Hey, Cap. Albandian's name showed up in the hitman circles using the code name Ophidian. I asked Pete to look him up, and he found the guy had an assignment to kill Arnold and his contact for the job was a woman named Barbara, which coincidently happens to be Mrs. Bayer's first name. I'm going to run over to the sister's and pick her up and book her for felony conspiracy."

'No, Sturgeon. You're not. Keep working at that site and gather as much evidence as you can. I'll talk to the ADA and see what she thinks. If that's enough for an arrest, I'll call you back. If I don't, you may assume it's a no."

"We're giving her a good deal of opportunity to book, Cap. If she finds out Albandian's been arrested, she'll do just that. She will find out, the media being the media."

"I'm aware of that, and I thank you for bringing me up to speed on something I already knew, but the answer remains the same. Stay on site."

"Geez, Crabby. Fine. I'll wait here for your call." Willow ended the call and put her phone back in her pocket. Obviously, Travis must have soured the captain's mood.

Daine

Vicki continued her work, outlining her case against Albandian, crossing all her t's and dotting all her i's. The more she got done today, the less she would have to work on over the holiday. Benny was off today. He was working hard at home preparing everything for tomorrow's dinner. She had struck gold when she married him. He had not disappointed her once. They had two children together, and he was not only a good husband, he was an excellent father.

It was not uncommon for an attorney to marry another attorney. Vicki had never met an attorney she could see herself married to, however. She had met Benjamin Daine at college. She was studying law and he was studying to become a doctor. They each had fulfilled their dreams. She was an ADA and he had his own oncology practice.

They were two totally different personalities, which was probably why they had so few marital problems. She was driven. Success was everything to her. Losing brought her to the pits of doom. He was passive. He pretty much had to be, considering his area of practice. There wasn't a lot of certainty treating cancer. He wasn't a quitter, though. He exhausted every avenue available to him and he read more than anyone she knew. He was always trying to find a better way. A more certain way.

Thanksgiving dinner was at their house, this year. Her brother and his family of four, and her mom and dad would be joining them. With her brother, Tom, living in Kansas City, it wasn't every year they could attend, which was why dinner was at the Daine residence. Her parents' place was just too small.

That would be tomorrow, though. Today, she still had work to do. The doctor at the hospital had said Albandian was at a recovery stage. All the broken bones had been set. Casts were in place, where needed, and pain medication was at a minimum.

Having heard that, she immediately called for transport. She called an ambulance and had called the captain, asking for an escort. He provided two. Albandian was now recovering in the medical wing of the county jail. It would be nice if the officers found something useful at his house, so she could arrange an arrest and a lineup. She didn't have enough, right now, but she had confidence they would find her something. Carpel's Crime Scene Unit was the best in the state. Her intercom buzzed and she answered. "Yes?"

"Vic, Captain Carson is on line three."

"Okay. Thank you."

Vicki felt her heart race. There wasn't a great deal of reasons that the captain would call her this close to the holiday, unless he had some news he thought she would need before Monday. For the sake of her guys, she wanted that news to be a connection between Albandian and Mrs.

Bayer. She mentally crossed her fingers and pushed line three.

"This is Vicki," she said with a little more eagerness than she'd intended.

"Vicki, this is Chet Carson. I've just heard from Detective Sturgeon. She said our Social guy looked up Albandian and found his search result indicated he accepted the Bayer hit and his contact was a woman named Barbara. That is the wife's name, by the way. Is that enough for Sturgeon to pick her up?"

Dammit, Vicki thought. "To pick her up? Yes, but what are you going to do with her when you do? Any attorney can blow that out of the water at trial. It is enough for a line-up, though. If we bring her in this close to a holiday, we need considerably more or the judge might be tempted toward empathy with her.

"I appreciate the call," Vicki continued, "but I really need something concrete. Hard evidence. If your man found a last name, as well, that would be different. Unfortunately, there are a lot of Barbara's out there. It's good supporting evidence, and I'll use it, but I need more. I know that sounds gluttonous, but that's the way the system works."

"Not to worry," the captain replied. "They're not leaving until they've covered everything. I know the CSU lead. She's relentless. If there's anything there, she'll find it."

"I appreciate that, Captain. Thank you so much for the call. My guys are sitting on her, right now, and I'd love to tell them to go home to their families. Please call, anytime."

"Will do," the captain responded and hung up after goodbyes were exchanged.

Vicki needed to find a way to get this ended before end of day. Right now, even probable cause would be questioned. Time was running out. Once the holiday was over, the feds would be all over Albandian. There would be a whirlwind of their own negotiations, and her leverage would disappear. Albandian was toast. Barbara Bayer, not so much. Vicki had a lot of tricks to get Mrs. Bayer to stand a line-up, but her attorney would simply tell the judge of the deception and any judge would dismiss the line-up results.

An ideal situation for Vicki would be if Mrs. Bayer offered to meet with the detectives, voluntarily, at the station. Vicki would simply bring Albandian in and positively identify her. Vicki, however, wasn't going to hold her breath on that one. Especially since she had alienated Birch. He would be less inclined to help her out. Detectives were no different from any other police officers, in that they stuck together like glue, so her chances of getting his partner to help her were just as slim.

If the word of a mass-murderer held any water, she would simply set it up, but Albandian's word that Mrs. Bayer had hired him was about as substantial as eating soup with a fork. She continued, mentally crossing her fingers for a breakthrough. It worked. Dave charged through the door, holding his pairing phone.

"Vic, there's a number on this phone listed as the Bayer client. It's the land line for the Bayer house. The date and time are two days prior to the killing. Saturday morning."

Vicki looked at the phone to verify for herself. Then she picked up her own phone and called Jerry. He answered.

"Happy friggin' Thanksgiving, Vic."

"It really is, Jerry. Pick her up. We got her."

"No shit? You don't have to tell me twice. We're on our way to the door right now. Your early Christmas present should be at County within a half hour."

"I'll be there to meet you." Vicki hung up and immediately called the county detention facility. When the man answered, she identified herself, briefed him, instructed him to have Albandian ready in the view port, and told him she would be there in fifteen.

Sturgeon

Willow wasn't all that certain there was anything here. She and Stan were on their second run-through of the bagged items on the table. He was rechecking her search and she was rechecking his. She hadn't seen or heard from Tara in over an hour, but there was a good number of weapons to sift through and log. She probably wouldn't see the woman for another hour.

This was a pretty big house and would take some time to completely canvas. CSU was still everywhere. There was one still in the back yard, two in the armory shed, one in the garage and three covering the assorted rooms. There was a man working on Albandian's computer and another in the living area, and a woman in the kitchen. Willow thought of asking for a cup of coffee, but didn't know the woman, or her capacity for humor.

This wasn't Willow's favorite part of the job. It was boring. She would much rather be out trying to talk Mrs. Bayer into confessing, but that obviously wasn't going to happen. In truth, about ninety percent of detective work was boring. When she was a patrolman, there was, at least, something different each day. Was she trying to convince herself to return to the streets?

A detective's pay was better and the prestige was sure there but she had never been much on prestige, and as far as the pay, she had invested well, being single. Money wasn't the draw. So why was she still a detective?

Her phone rang, breaking up all of her 'woe me' thoughts. It was the captain. "Sturgeon."

"Sturgeon, do you want to have a little fun?" Willow didn't think the captain had worded that question all that well, but she let it slide to find out what fun he had in mind.

"Sure. Will it get me off this boring job?" Two could play the word-play game.

"It will. The ADA is having Mrs. Bayer picked up. She will be arrested and taken to County. If you hurry, you can be there when she's brought in. Have Sims give his squad keys to Tara. One of them can bring it in. If the ADA doesn't ask the why question, make sure you do."

"I'm there. Leaving now." She put her phone back in her pocket and turned to Stan.

"Give your unit keys to Tara. We're leaving." Willow almost laughed as Stan nearly ran through the garage before she had finished. Apparently, she wasn't the only one who was bored.

Willow gathered her things and headed out the door. Stan caught up before she reached it. The trip to County wouldn't take all that long but she started a conversation with Stan nonetheless. She wanted to know as much about him as possible, in the event their paths crossed again.

Stan related he had become a police officer because it was in the family. He had originally come from Portland, Oregon, and his father and grandfather were on the force there. Neither of them had progressed beyond sergeant, and he hoped to eclipse that someday. He had been hired last month, and had been in the top three in testing. He was married, with a one-year-old daughter. His education, in its entirety, had been in Oregon. He had met his wife there, but she lived in Carpel, which prompted the move here.

There were questions asked and answers given, and the time passed quickly. Willow pulled into the County lot and found a spot immediately. The two hurried into the lobby and found a woman decked out in a business skirt and blouse and heels. This had to be the ADA. Willow was a little bit intimidated, but not by her position. This was a beautiful woman. There wasn't a single hair out of place. She approached and identified herself.

"Counselor Daine, I'm guessing? I'm Detective Willow Sturgeon, and this is Officer Stan Sims. I hope you don't mind if we watch," Willow said, offering her hand.

"Not at all," the ADA responded, accepting both hands. Willow found the handshake firm and confident.

"I'm surprised not to see your partner," the ADA continued. "I was sure he'd be here before me, even."

"He took the rest of the day off," Willow offered, but didn't elaborate. The pained expression on the ADA's face surprised Willow. It almost looked like guilt. She was tempted to dig for information but she wasn't sure she should mess with an ADA.

"We're ready, Counselor," a deputy said as he entered the room.

"Thank you," she responded and then turned to Willow and Stan. "Officer Sims, I'll have to ask you to join me, away from the entry. Detective, if you will, I would like to ask you to sit at this table and face the view port with these other two nice ladies. We're going to ask Albandian if you were the one that hired him."

Humor. Willow loved it. "I'll sit right here and put on my best guilty face. He's already seen me, though. I interviewed him."

"Well, that's actually a good thing. If he picks you out, we'll know he's full of shit. Cora, give the detective one of the wigs, please."

One of the ladies sitting at the table reached down and pulled out a couple of wigs from a bag. Willow had wondered what she would look like as a redhead, so she chose that one and took a seat with the others. She placed the wig, positioned it properly, checked herself in her mirror, and waited for the show to begin.

Daine

Vicki led Officer Sims into the view room, where they stood waiting for Jerry and Alan to arrive with Mrs. Bayer. It wasn't much of a wait. Alan walked in with the handcuffed Mrs. Bayer and sat her at the table with the other three women. He said something to the other three and they all moved their hands behind their backs. Mrs. Bayer looked distraught so the other three put on like expressions. Jerry entered and made his way to the view room.

"I don't know, Vic," he said as he entered. "Are you sure about the date and time of their meeting you gave me? She's pretty insistent she was in Palo Alto that whole weekend. We told her we would verify that, but she stuck to her story."

"Did you verify?"

"I tried, but the woman is out of the office for the weekend. They said they'd call her at home and have her call me, but I haven't received anything yet. I didn't tell Mrs. Albandian she was sitting a line-up."

"Who is the other woman?"

"That's her sister. She's going to either bail Mrs. Albandian out or if she's not arrested, drive her home.

What are your thoughts if the Palo Alto woman calls me back?"

"Doesn't matter," Vicki said. "We're about to blow her alibi out of the water anyway." Vicki looked at the deputy and nodded. The deputy left and returned shortly with a wheelchair-bound Albandian.

"When was the last time you took a pain pill, Mr. Albandian?" Vicki asked.

"About three hours ago, and the pain is back, so let's get this over with."

"We will. I want you to look through this window at the ladies sitting at the table. They're not holding numbers, so I want you to go from left to right. The woman on the left will be number one and the woman on the right will be number four. You pick her out. Tell me a number. A hair color and a shirt color. Do you have any questions?"

"No. Thank you for thinking I'm an idiot, though."

"You ended the life of several human beings, Mr. Albandian. You robbed their families of your victims' love. And for what? Money? Money that sits in an off-shore account and will never be had by you? Put there because you had the audacity to think you would never get caught? You are the worst kind of idiot." Vicki pointed at the window. Albandian was wheeled over. He looked at the women and then back at Vicki.

"Is this supposed to be funny, or are you the idiot? None of them."

Vicki was losing her patience. "I can make what's left of your life a living hell, Mr. Albandian. Mrs. Bayer is at that table. Look again."

"I don't have to look again. None of those women hired me," he snarled. Jerry grabbed his ear and twisted it. Albandian screamed in pain. "Alright, alright. I'll look again."

"Good, Mr. Albandian," Vicki said. "Because if this is some kind of assassin code, I have a code of my own."

Albandian looked through the window a second time and immediately began shaking his head. He stopped shaking and stared through the glass. He stared for several seconds and then turned to look at Vicki. "She's there, but she's not at the table."

Vicki walked to the window and peered through, Jerry immediately putting himself between her and Albandian. There was one other woman in the room. She was standing against the wall, talking to Alan, but facing the table.

"Are you telling me that the woman talking to the man is the one who hired you?"

"Yup. Clever trick on your part, though. Making me focus on the women at the table. Mrs. Bayer is the one standing against the wall."

Vicki looked at Jerry. "It looks like Mrs. Bayer's alibi is sound. Release her. Who is that woman?"

"Charlotte Jergens. Mrs. Bayer's sister."

"Hook her up. Book her. Let her stew in a cell for the night. We'll start the investigation Friday. What a horrible thing to do to your sister."

Sturgeon

Willow watched as the ADA's investigator came out of the back and went right to Mrs. Bayer. At first, she thought they had a positive ID, but then she became confused as the investigator removed the handcuffs from Mrs. Bayer and told her she was free to go, apologizing that this happened to her. Why would he apologize?

The investigator walked over to her sister and said something to her. The sister looked defiant at first, but then turned around and put her hands against the wall. Willow got it. Mrs. Bayer's husband had been killed by her sister. What a bitch. They were obviously waiting for a female deputy for a frisk, and Willow was about to volunteer. Before she could, Mrs. Bayer interrupted her thoughts.

"What's going on with Char?" she asked with a very confused look. Willow wasn't about to tell her, but as it turned out, she didn't need to. Mrs. Bayer apparently figured it out as well. Willow bolted at her, but she was too slow. Mrs. Bayer whizzed by her, charging her sister.

"YOU KILLED ARNIE?" she screamed, reaching her. The investigator's attempts to intervene were likewise too slow. Mrs. Bayer grabbed her sister's hair, pulling her from the wall. She began pummeling her sister's face with her right fist, while holding the hair with her left. The sister's knees buckled from the blows and she collapsed to the floor.

Willow reached Mrs. Bayer and bulldogged her to the floor in an attempt to separate her from her sister. Mrs. Bayer continued to swing and didn't let go of the hair, so the cuffed woman was dragged several feet. Willow pulled the swinging right away, pinning it against Mrs. Bayer's side, while the investigator attempted to separate the left from the hair.

Mrs. Bayer was strong. She wasn't releasing her grip on the hair. She switched to screaming and began kicking out at her sister. Another man, presumably also an investigator, sat on Mrs. Bayer's legs, rendering them useless. Willow attempted to calm her down, but the rage and fury she saw in the woman's eyes told her it would be futile. Mrs. Bayer began violently jerking the hair. The head flew freely. Her sister was unconscious from one of Mrs. Bayer's blows.

The female deputy had come in earlier, but then went back to the back area. Now she re-emerged carrying a pair of scissors. She knelt beside the sister and began to cut the woman's hair away from Mrs. Bayer's grip. Mrs. Bayer, seeing what was happening, released her grip to get a better one, but the deputy, seeing this, grabbed Mrs. Bayer's arm and twisted it against her back. Willow locked the arm against her side, and with her free legs began scooting Mrs. Bayer along the tiled floor, away from her sister.

Mrs. Bayer's rage turned to frustration and she began screaming obscenities and threats toward her sister. With the help of the second investigator, they had her pinned pretty well. Willow looked over at the limp figure on the floor, now being attended to by medical personnel.

As she surveyed the area, she saw the ADA standing and talking with the two other women who had sat the lineup, probably from her office, all watching the scene unfold. Stan was there, as well. Willow thought of thanking him for his help, but there wasn't really any way she could have squeezed in. It was clogged enough. The original investigator was standing over the prone sister and medical personnel. The female deputy was frisking her, and a gurney was being wheeled in from the back.

Attempts to revive the sister were futile. She was out cold. They loaded her on the gurney and wheeled her into the back, with the deputy following. Willow heard the click of the lock and she and the investigator removed themselves from Mrs. Bayer, jumping quickly away, so as not to be reached by that right cross.

Mrs. Bayer stayed on the floor, bawling into the tile. The ADA walked over and went down beside her, stroking her hair and uttering soothing words. As if there were any soothing words that would help in this situation. What a horrid sequence of events. Your husband killed by your sister.

Willow knew she had to call the captain, but she didn't have an answer to the question he would ask, and she didn't see any way she would any time soon. Perhaps, if the ADA had any success calming down Mrs. Bayer, she would be able to enlighten them on why Mr. Bayer had been targeted.

Willow hoped she would be able to give Travis some good news. She knew there was no way he would consider the case closed until he had the why question answered. All the speculation in the world wouldn't help calm him.

The ADA helped Mrs. Bayer off the floor and sat her in one of the chairs. The two women who had sat the table with Willow joined them. They, too, were consoling Mrs. Bayer. Willow took the opportunity to corral the ADA. She walked over to get her attention, and the ADA got the picture and excused herself, walking away with Willow.

Remembering the look of guilt on the ADA's face when she was told Travis had taken the rest of the day off, she asked her questions. "Is it possible to talk to you a moment, and maybe Mrs. Bayer as well? My partner has had a rough start to his Thanksgiving, and I would like to cheer him up, if I can."

"I'm not sure about Mrs. Bayer, but how can I help you?"

"Travis is in a very distraught state right now. He thinks the reason we were denied access to Albandian's phone was because there were pictures of his family on it. Is that accurate?"

"I'm not sure I'm the one to discuss that, Detective. I think you should speak with the captain."

"So that's a yes, then," Willow surmised, trying to hide a saddened expression. The ADA didn't want to lie, and she knew Willow had figured the truth out. Then she elaborated.

"Look, Detective. Yes, there were pictures on the phone, but they weren't live pictures. They were pictures of pictures. The defendant had obviously been in Detective Birch's residence and taken photos of some framed pictures displayed around his home. The captain was concerned about the detective's reaction if he found out, so he asked for my discretion."

"I can understand that, I guess. I think the captain is wrong, but he does know Travis better than I," Willow responded as she realized those pictures had probably been taken when Travis was having his love connection with the bottle. He may have even been in the house, but passed out drunk at the time. That would help her calm him down about it. He already knew he was a mess at that time, so he would probably agree with her.

"I'll get confirmation from the captain," Willow added. "That way he won't know you squealed."

The ADA actually laughed. It was the first time Willow had even seen a smile from the woman. "I'm not concerned about the captain thinking I squealed. I'm pretty sure I can take him."

This time Willow laughed. Then she changed her focus to Mrs. Bayer. She pointed. "May I?"

"Give it a shot. I need her, though, so I may stop you at some point."

"Fair enough." Willow walked over and asked the ADA staff to give her the chairs. She sat down and placed her hand on Mrs. Bayer's shoulder as the ADA took another chair beside them.

"I'm so sorry this happened to you, Mrs. Bayer. It is certainly an awful development. Do you feel like answering a couple of questions for me?"

"No. I probably never will, though, so ask away."

"It's pretty obvious from your reaction this was quite a surprise to you. If I may ask, though, do you have any idea why your sister would want to harm your husband?"

"I know exactly why," Mrs. Bayer related with conviction. She began sobbing again, so Willow had to wait a bit for the answer. Once Mrs. Bayer gathered herself enough to speak again, she continued, "She and Tom are flat-broke and always borrowing money. He's worthless. He can't hold a job more than a month."

After a short pause caused by sniffling and nose blowing, she continued, "Arnie was fed up with the guy and told Char he wasn't supporting them anymore. With

Arnie dead, the store would revert to me. I've never really had an interest, and she knew that. She's been after me to move back to Kansas and let her take care of the store. She's been saying that staying here would always remind me of Arnie and I needed to move on."

"Would you have done that, Mrs. Bayer?" the ADA asked.

"Probably. I really have no idea how to operate a store. She's been in business before, but the dumbass drank all her profits. I had really felt bad about Arnie's decision. I felt sorry for her." Mrs. Bayer's facial expression turned sour. "What an evil bitch she has become, living with that man."

"Financial stress can cause some to take drastic steps," the ADA responded. "Although, I'm not sure I've heard of steps that drastic."

"What will you do, now?" Willow asked.

"I don't know. I probably will move back home. There sure as hell isn't anything left here for me. She was my only sibling, and our kids are grown and moved away."

"I may have a half-way good idea, if you're interested," Willow interjected. "It will be your decision, naturally, but Mr. Bayer's staff at the store are very good at what they do. Selling the store outright, right away, might be something you'll regret later. They could run the store for you, and you wouldn't have to get involved any more than you want to."

"I'll think about it. I'm not sure yet. I'm still reeling from Arnie's death. . . and now this."

"I understand. I'll give you the number of a young lady who worked there. I've come to know her pretty well. I know she'll help you with whatever you decide. All the employees will. They were pretty fond of your husband."

"Can we give you a ride home?" the ADA asked as Willow was writing Gracie's phone number down.

"I should just take her car. It's not like she's going to be needing it."

"I don't think that car is still here," the ADA said, looking at her investigator. He shook his head and the ADA continued, "That car's been towed, Mrs. Bayer. Jerry will give you a ride."

"I don't mean to tell you your job, Counselor, but you might want to look into that shithead. I wouldn't be surprised if he was involved, somehow."

"I will do that."

Willow handed Mrs. Bayer Gracie's phone number and then Jerry escorted the grieving woman out to the parking lot. Willow stayed seated with the ADA and then offered her opinion.

"I wouldn't be surprised if the man was very much involved, based on her description."

"You can bet I'll find out if he was." The two shook hands and Willow left for her own car.

Thanksgiving

Sturgeon

Willow let Pepper out one last time, as she waited for Mark to arrive. She filled the water dishes and food dishes, placing Salt's food on the top tier of his cat tree, which was her usual practice when she would be gone for a while. Pepper had a tendency to borrow some of Salt's food, which was easy to correct when she was home but difficult when she wasn't.

While Pepper was attending to business, she made one more pass through the house to make sure all the windows and doors were locked and the reading room door closed, a practice she had been forced into one day, when she'd learned of Salt's fascination with books. Ripping them apart, as opposed to reading them.

With everything as it should be, she let Pepper back in, locked the slider, grabbed her purse and the mincemeat pie she had made and went to the front door to wait. She didn't even make it that far, as Mark came through carrying her sweater that she had left at his house. She donned it, attached her off-duty to her hip, and they were off for their first Thanksgiving dinner.

This would be the first of three. The Birch dinner would be the standard turkey dinner. The good news about this Thanksgiving was that, for once, she would be doing no cooking. She would help, naturally, but there wouldn't be any laboring in the kitchen all day.

Kris was a very good cook. Willow had already been blessed with her meals, and the woman knew her way around spices. For the dinner at her parents' house, her dad did the cooking, and he didn't like anyone in the kitchen when he was cooking. As for the Gaudiers, it was, surprisingly, all Missy. Lauren had said when she had been teaching the kids how to cook that they all learned well but Missy had really excelled, and apparently it was more instinct than Lauren's teaching.

"Don't you dare make any sharp turns or stops! My pie is on the floor," Willow quipped at Mark as they seated themselves in his car.

"Yes, dear," Mark replied, practicing the proper response she had given him to any statement she would ever make.

"That-a-boy," she said as they both shared a laugh.

The conversation during the drive was centered around the wedding, trying to decide on a date. Willow was a little reluctant to think much beyond that, as she had decided to take Amy's advice and talk to Lauren about being her wedding planner. Never having been married before, or having a wedding planner, she had admitted to herself she had no idea how much a wedding planner needed to be involved in decisions.

There was a good deal of down time as each of them wrestled with their own thoughts about the best-case scenario as far as dates went. It wasn't all Willow was thinking about, though. Her mind wandered to her past all the way back to her childhood. Picnics in the park when she was five. Campouts in the backyard when she was eight. Finally getting her very own room when she was seven and not having to smell her brother's stinky farts.

Her graduation from grammar school to middle school and a whole new circle of friends. Her best friend, Cece, moving to Florida and never being heard from again. Trips to the grocery store with Mom. Just the two of them. She remembered trying to make money selling lemonade, so she could buy her favorite Back Street Boys CD. She remembered how much her dad laughed when he handed her a CD by the Beetles and she had asked who they were.

At the time of her childhood there was nothing that made her feel better than when one or both of her parents laughed. The harder they laughed, the better she felt. No amount of time she spent with her friends, zoo trips, carnival rides or any other childhood activity could compare to hearing her parents happy.

Then that dreadful day came. The day he walked into the house carrying that ugly brown bottle. The laughter had ended and was replaced by screaming that had been so loud the neighbors had called the police. Day after day. Week after week, it had gotten worse. She and her brother had been shipped off to Aunt Vic's.

Aunt Vic had never talked about what was going on with her mom and dad. Willow had feared they were getting divorced, and she had cried herself to sleep most nights.

Luck was with her and her brother, though. The arguments had been long and loud, she had found out later. Mom had thrown her dad out, but that lasted about ten minutes. It was a wake-up call for him, however. It was a life-altering wake-up call.

Dad had joined the local AA. Aunt Vic had taken them home. There was a long period of reserved behavior on her mom's part toward her dad. Willow and her brother had worked hard to get them laughing again. It had taken months before she had heard her dad laugh, and over a year to hear her mom. It was never again the same laughter, however.

Now she was getting married. She was starting a family and she was frightened, like never before. What kind of parent would she be? She had no idea. What kind of wife? Fear was not something she was accustomed to experiencing. She was certainly feeling it now. She was jolted from her thoughts as she realized Mark had asked her a question. Should he bring wine for turkey dinner at her parents'?

"I don't think so. Mom hates wine and Dad won't drink it. I'll do another pie. Dad loves pumpkin pie. I'll make one of those."

When it came to parenting, she and Mark differed on the most important decision there would ever be for parents. Biological or adoption. She wanted children, but Mark was and always had been passionate about all the children out there without homes. He wanted to provide them with a home. Not a house. A home. She loved his kindness, but she knew there was going to have to be a compromise. She just wasn't sure how many children he had in mind. She would like two, but men usually wanted more. A topic for another day. Mark pulled to a stop in front of the Birch residence.

She looked down at her pie, and it was still there. Good job, Mark. She picked it up and exited the car. She and Mark walked to the door. Knowing they were expected, she opened the door and announced herself with a hello.

"We're in the kitchen," Kris informed them. "The boys are in the den watching football."

Birch

Travis heard the sounds coming from down the hall and realized Mark and Willow were there. The Lions were on the ten-yard line, so he left the television on so that Ashton could watch his favorite team find a way not to get the ball in the end zone. He made his way out of the den to greet his guests.

"Hey, Mark," he greeted with a handshake. "Lions are playing the Bears, if you want to partake," he finished, pointing down the hall. He walked past Mark to the kitchen where Willow was talking with Kris, with Macy attached to her leg.

"Happy Thanksgiving, partner," he said. "Macy, leave the poor woman's leg alone, please."

"Oh, she's alright," Willow responded, stroking Macy's hair.

"Say, Will," Travis continued, "did you learn anything about the guy's phone?"

"Oh. Okay. We'll jump right into this, then. Let's go out back."

"Yeah, sorry," Travis said, leading the way out the back slider. Macy climbed back up on her chair, supervising her mom's cooking. "I just have a concern about the contents." He walked to the steps leading down to the yard and turned to face her. Instead of telling him what he wanted to know, she stiff-armed him hard in the chest, sending him down the three steps and sprawling on the grass.

"What the hell is wrong with you, Willow? What's that all about?"

"Don't ever hang up on me again. Ever." Her expression was one that convinced him it wasn't a playful jab. She was genuinely pissed.

"I'm sorry, Will. I was just. . ." Before he could complete his sentence, she held up a finger.

"I don't give a rat's ass what your excuse is."

"Okay, then. I'm sorry I hung up on you. Now tell me what was so important that we couldn't see the phone."

"Yeah. About that," she began, but instead of telling him, she turned and walked back into the house.

Yup. She was pissed, alright. He'd hung up on her and now she was hanging up her info on him. He followed her back into the house and she was again talking to Kris. Calmly, as if she hadn't just sent the woman's husband hunting worms.

"Forgot your nightstick, I see," Kris said to Willow with a smile.

"Decided I didn't need it. He's lost a lot of weight, but there's still a small paunch there."

"You do see me standing here, right?" Travis announced to the two.

"I see you standing now, yes," Kris said, stifling a laugh.

"Very funny," Travis responded. He knew if his family was in danger, Willow wouldn't be playing this game, so he guessed the contents of the phone weren't pictures of Kris and the kids out and about. He just grumbled under his breath and went back to the den and the more pleasant company of Mark and Ashton.

When he entered, Mark was on the couch, Ashton still on the floor, and the ball now belonging to the Bears. No change in the score. Not even a field goal. Unbelievable. He took a seat in his chair and asked Ashton what had happened.

"Fourth and goal at the two, and they went for it, Dad. A tie score in the first half and they went for it. The coach is stupid."

"Hey, mister," Travis said. "Don't let your mother hear you use that word."

"What word should I use?" Ashton asked.

"The coach is in need of advice," Travis answered.

"You know why he needs advice, Dad?" Ashton asked.

Travis gave his son a disapproving look, knowing full well he was going to say the coach is in need of advice because he's stupid. Ashton just turned and watched the game, dropping the matter. Travis looked over at Mark and the man was beet red, trying to keep from laughing.

"How goes the decision on a wedding date?" Travis asked.

"Don't know yet," Mark answered. "Apparently, she's going to be turning the planning over to Lauren Gaudier. We're going there this weekend, too. I'll know more Monday."

"Wow. She has really gotten close to that family. Good for her."

"Oh. I think Willow gets along with just about anyone. She's a great personality."

"You should have been in the back yard a few minutes ago," Travis replied. Mark gave him a querulous look, but Travis just shook him off and went back to the game talk. During the talk, Travis was trying to determine the best method to get Willow to tell him what was so confidential about the killer's phone. Even though he knew she wouldn't keep things from him that would endanger his family, he still wanted to know what the big deal was. Maybe after she calmed down about being hung up on.

Macy entered the room and announced that dinner was ready. Travis sent Ashton in to be the first to wash up, Macy darted back to help with table setting, and Travis took the opportunity to ask Mark for his thoughts on asking Willow.

"Let me ask you, Mark, before we go to the table. I made the mistake of hanging up on Will, and she didn't take it well. As a result, she is holding back on some information I asked for. Any advice on how to calm the waters?"

"Well, as for women in general, my advice would be to never hang up on one. Any woman. In the history of the telephone. For time eternal. It's the equivalent of telling an angry woman to calm down. Same basic effect. Same response. As for Willow, my advice would be to leave me out of it. You stuck your foot in the mud. I'm certainly not going to pull it out for you."

"Well, you're worthless," Travis said with a smile.

"In this regard, I agree."

After washing up, themselves, Mark and Travis proceeded to the table and found everyone sitting and waiting. Kris offered to let the guests say grace, and Willow volunteered. The dinner was exceptional, as always with Kris. Travis was careful not to overindulge, and when dinner was finished, he began cleaning dishes.

While doing so, he noticed the kids had retired to their games, Kris and Mark were sitting in the living room, talking about the wedding, and Willow was behind Travis, staring at him.

"Kris is a good cook, isn't she?" he asked with a smile.

"She certainly is," Willow said as she picked up a towel and began to help.

"You don't have to do that, Willow. Go visit. I've got this."

She didn't move and kept drying dishes. She was obviously wrestling with her thoughts. After a short time, she just blurted it out.

"There were pictures of the inside of your house on Albandian's phone." Willow paused and Travis froze. Then she continued, "I've looked and I can tell you the pictures aren't recent. All the picture frames are out of place. The house is a mess. There's a pizza box on the couch and an empty glass on the coffee table. He had obviously broken in when you were on your bender. You may have even been here, although with as cocky as the guy was, probably not. He would have just shot you and been done with it.

"According to the ADA," she continued, "he is also the killer in a cold case you had been working on. He probably thought you were getting too close and was looking for leverage."

There was another pause. Travis kept silent and waited. Inside, he was fuming that the captain had kept this from him. Everyone had, actually. Everyone but Willow. She continued.

"Mrs. Bayer wasn't the person who had hired him. It was her sister, Charlotte. He picked her out in front of the ADA and several witnesses. She'll be gone for a while, anyway. Just before I went to bed, last night, I received a text from the captain. The ADA is very good. The sister confessed. She wanted the store and she knew Mrs. Bayer didn't and would have signed it over to her."

There were several moments of silence. He saw Willow looking at him a couple of times during the silence. He was thankful for her. Thankful that he had at least one friend who would tell him the truth.

"Thank you, Will. Thanks for telling me and thanks for, apparently, being my only friend in the department."

"How do you come upon that, Travis?"

"Friendship is the person who tells you the truth of the matter."

"Bullshit! Friendship is caring, Travis. Giving a damn. Friendship is not allowing you to become so incensed you do something stupid. Friendship is caring enough about you to keep you safe from losing your job when you go on a tirade after finding out the man had been in your house. You have more friends than you think you do, and you have to stop thinking you're the only one in the world who can fix things. Everything about this was handled perfectly to keep you from being an idiot. From Laticia to Tara, to the captain, and especially to ADA Daine. They care, Travis. They cared about you. Not the phone. Not Albandian."

"It's still hard to swallow."

"Then start chewing harder. You scared that poor Laticia girl to death. You owe a lot of apologies. You need to understand you have a lot of help. Use it. Be kinder.

Above all, stop with the 'our case' crap. We're a team. All of us." Willow sat the towel down and put her hand on his shoulder. "Give me a hug."

"That's not appropriate."

She squeezed his shoulder to make sure he was looking in her eyes. He did. "Never use that word again. It's the dumbest word to use with a friend. Friends don't have to be appropriate. That's why they're friends. Now give me a hug, or I'm going to smack you."

Travis dried his hands and placed them around Willow and pulled her tight. Partner. Friend. Confidant.

Epilogue

Zachary "Zack" Albandian was found guilty and sentenced to twenty-two consecutive sentences of life in prison without the possibility of parole. He wasn't able to enjoy the luxury promised him by Victoria Daine, however. He was murdered his second day in prison while eating in the mess hall.

ADA Daine agreed to drop the murder charge if Charlotte Jergens pleaded guilty to conspiracy to commit murder. She did and was sentenced to twenty years without the possibility of parole. Furious with the sentence, Jergens told the judge she found one and could find another. The judge added ten years to her sentence so she would have time for research.

Barbara Bayer did indeed decide to retain Arnold's Discount. However, she moved as she said she would, and appointed Grace Blankenship to the position of General Manager.

Soldier Jack continues to be homeless, by choice, and continues to provide a service to the assorted businesses in Historical in return for whatever they feel fair.

Gracie Blankenship spent all her spare time working with the VA on Jack's behalf, providing transportation to and from the VA for him to tell his story and request benefits. Jack has dinner at Gracie's every Sunday evening.

Victoria Daine received a commendation from the city for the conviction, and the DA refused the press release she had prepared, telling her to contact the press herself. She did, and not once in the release, did she use the word I, instead giving credit to the Carpel Police Department, her investigators, her staff and 'two thumbs-up' for detectives Birch and Sturgeon.

Lauren Gaudier happily agreed to be Willow and Mark's wedding planner. The date was set for June 27th. The reception was to be held at the Gaudier mansion. Willow and Amy spent the next week looking at dresses before Amy had to return to school.

And Travis Birch? Well, he was becoming less intense and more personable, thanks to his association with Willow, and now her fiancé Mark. Willow had become a friend, not just a partner. Her relationship with Mark had been good for Travis, as well. The two exchanged barbs nearly every time they would meet. Mark would continue to ask Travis questions that would make the man uncomfortable. "If your wife asks you how you like her hair, how do you respond?" To which Travis would laughingly say, "It looks like a hornet's nest."

He and Mark would laugh heartily, until Willow and Kris came in to the room with smiles wanting to know what was funny. Travis would stumble for words, and Mark would rat him out. The banter actually loosened Travis up and his interviews became more cordial and less intense.

Willow and Birch were becoming stronger as a team with each case.